CW00662312

ORON AMULAR

BOOK 1: THE CALL OF THE MOUNTAIN

MICHAEL J HARVEY

malcolm down
PUBLISHING

Copyright © 2019 Michael J. Harvey

22 21 20 19 7 6 5 4 3 2 1

First published 2019 by Malcolm Down Publishing Ltd.
www.malcolmdown.co.uk

The right of Michael J Harvey to be identified as the author of this work has been asserted by him in accordance with the Copyright, Designs and Patents Act 1988.

All rights reserved. No part of this publication may be reproduced, stored in a retrieval system, or transmitted in any other form or by any means, electronic, mechanical, photocopying, recording or otherwise, without the prior permission of the publisher.

British Library Cataloguing in Publication Data
A catalogue record for this book is available from the British Library.

ISBN 978-1-912863-27-3

Original cover image by Arthur Dukes
Cover design by Esther Kotecha
Art direction by Sarah Grace

Printed in the UK

Oron Amular is dedicated to Nana,

my first and greatest fan.

I hope that somehow, somewhere,

you get to read this.

ACKNOWLEDGEMENTS

The love and support of many people has helped to bring *Oron Amular* into being. I owe a great debt of gratitude to those whose belief and encouragement sustained me in both the writing and the hunt for publication. I wish to thank my parents, Ian and Lucie, for raising me in a home of love and faith, and for setting my feet on this path. I reserve special thanks for Kelly Jamieson, for being so vocal a fan, right from the start, and for your friendship since. Phil Dobbs, it wasn't quite your thing, but you always encouraged me along the way, and never stopping asking about it. Pat Eisner and Matt Taylor also deserve my appreciation, for being among the first to read it, and for much practical support and helpful input. Many other friends have encouraged me hugely, too many to name, but you know who you are and I really appreciate it. I'm also really grateful to the whole team at Malcolm Down Publishing for taking this chance with me and bringing *Oron Amular* to print. No one has done more to make this novel possible, than my beloved wife, Lucy, my *Soleithébar*. Thank you for letting me have all those hours; thank you for believing in me; thank you for walking this road with me as the best of companions. Most of all, though, I wish to thank God, from whom comes every good and perfect gift (James 1:17). You gave me this imagination, these ideas, and this talent, and I honour You with every word that I write.

CONTENTS

Map of
Astrom
Icy Seas
Urunmar
Oron Cavardul
Troizon Ocean
Retorn Ocean
The Haunted Pass
Gulf of Urunumar
Tor Kenfer
Guard Hills
Ciricen
River Road
Lutetian
Rohandur
Centaur
Nalator
Hendar
River Gorathar
Osincos
Malator
Kalator
Beachbone Bay
Kalimar
Del Sereph
Porinar
River Goralar
Lalator
Oron Amular
Paeyeir
Hamid
Goragath Mountains
Firewood
White Mts
Dorzand
Black Mts
Marindel
Noir
Nimrell Bay
Aranar
Tol Ankil
Ithrill
White Hills
Cavalras
Silver City
River Elarim
Armist Road
Arkania Forest
Markest
Arke
Lancorin
Carthaki Mts
Arton
East Fold
Del Tharmar
Silver Bay
Phoenix
Maristonia
Swordhilt Peninsula
Welton
Carthak
Mariston
Dagger's Cove
Mariston Bay
West Fold
Mandoas
South Fold
Sapheil Ocean
Marble Bay
Raduthon
Lurallan
Urundair
Southern Cape
© Michael J Harvey

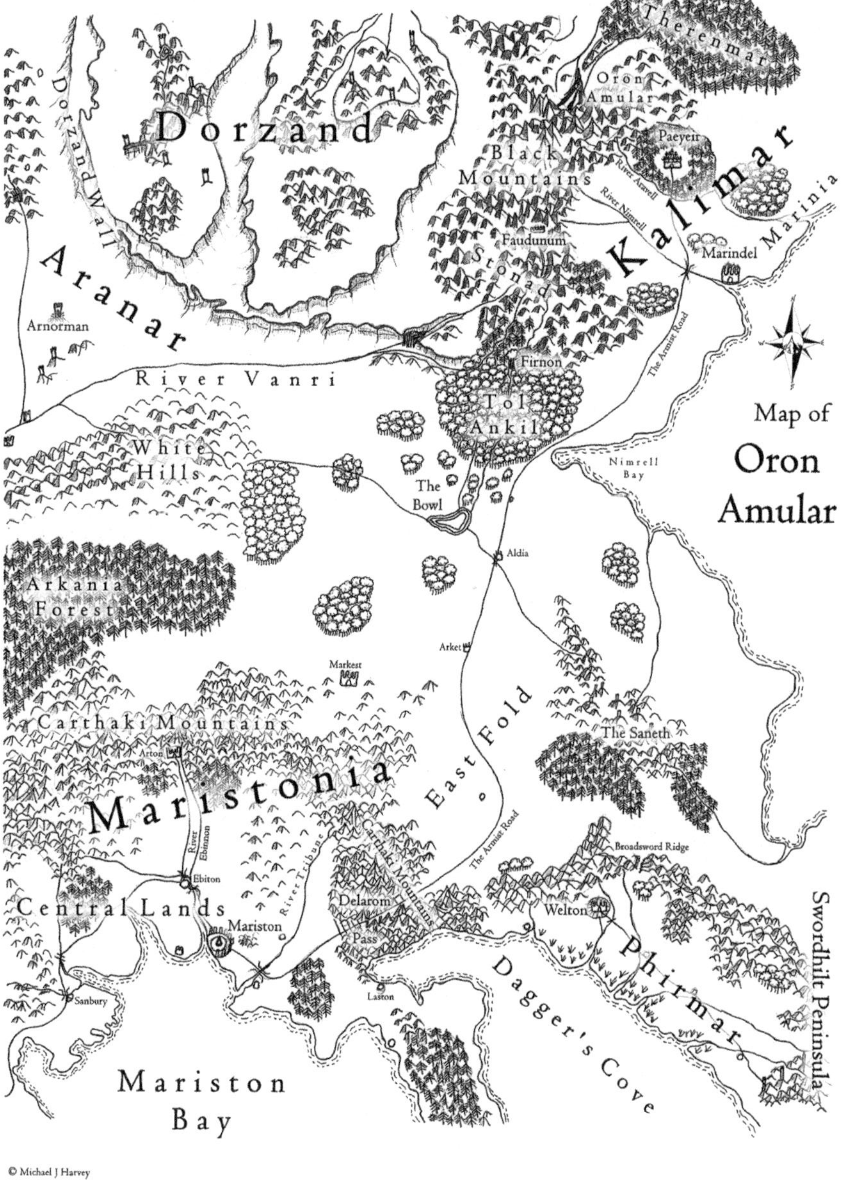

© Michael J Harvey

I
A Tournament

THIS was the day. Wasn't it? It must be. The thought kept him going as he climbed the hill during the night. He had been waiting for this day half his life. If his conviction were wrong, he wasn't sure he could carry on. He was at the summit in time to see the first hint of dawn colouring the sky behind the mountains in the east. He shivered as the wind blew away the last wisps of mist around him, leaving the view he had come for unimpeded. He was not disappointed. The tranquil violet of the slumbering world was blushed with peach as the sun peeped over the mountains. The light shifted imperceptibly through exquisite shades of rose and vermillion. As it did so, the landscape of tilled fields and little towns gradually took on definition. So too did the poplar-lined road, running east to west through it all. Settling down to wait, he watched the road.

The higher the sun rose, the more his eyes narrowed. Daylight imparted each contour of the land with a subtly unique tint of gold as it advanced westward, but the beauty of it was lost on him. His attention was fixed on the road. He would wait for the sign. He would wait all day if need be – but after that? He wasn't sure.

Fourscore years had given him patience, half of them spent in waiting. Yet an armist could not live on hopes and dreams forever. He was not yet past his prime, as some armists might view it, but he felt much older. Instead of the excitement and camaraderie which others of his age might have experienced, all he had ever known was sorrow, frustration and delay. He had spent forty years waiting upon a promise, clinging to a hope. His mane of red hair might look aflame in the waxing daylight, but the strength of that hope within was now scarce more than a flicker. He thought that today was the day. Or had he misread the sign? He had spent all his life in the mountains, had stood every night facing east. Hoping. Waiting. Willing. In his dreams, he had seen many times that towering flash of fire searing the mountain sky, so many times that when his waking eyes beheld it, he could not be sure that it had not been another dream after all.

If today was not the day, what would he do? He looked down at himself. The hose, tunic, coat and cloak which had once been such bright red and orange were now faded to dusty browns and yellows and a colour which looked depressingly like dried blood. His strong leather boots, studded with gripping nails, were starting to fall apart again. That's what came of constantly being on the move. Yet often he had nothing better to do than collect news of all kinds. He had no place to call his own; the only home he had ever known had been burned to the ground by bandits. So he simply wandered. Wandered from place to place and from town to town, seeking lodgings where he could or sleeping underneath the stars when no place could be found. Early on he had discovered that he could conjure and enchant like his father, and with the help of Prélan he had somehow managed to scratch a living. Some villages had shunned him as a vagabond, others had refused to let him stay after discovering what he could do, and even those few which paid for his entertainment soon grew weary of him and rarely had kind words to say. That had left him little choice but to mostly keep his own company. He had no one to call him friend. If he died here, casting himself from that high place, would anyone ever know?

Eyes squinting in the strengthening sunshine, he watched society begin to pulse in the world below him. Work parties tramped to the fields and merchant caravans plied the roads. Their life was so alien to him, bracketed as it was by the daily rhythms of purpose, and he understood them little. Overlong locks of reddish hair kept falling across his eyes, and time and again he brushed them away with his hand. Then he saw it. One puff of dust among many, as of a swift rider galloping along the highway, but there could be no mistaking what happened next. His eyes widened when, out from the dust-cloud, there bloomed a vision. It was the emblem of a foreign power. Silver runes and a conical mountain, all on a sable field. Within the mountain were successive roundels of different colours, whilst flanking it on either side was a staff, fire pouring from their tips. This banner mushroomed so large that it filled most of Roujeark's vision, allowing him to see every detail. His eyes were drawn especially to the device in the bottom corner of the vision: a six-pointed star with strange words beneath it: *ce avar kalanor, genmos ey ce corpide*. His father had taught him the elven characters, so he knew it said *the brightest star, first and the last*, but he had no idea what it meant. Yet there could be no mistaking it: this was the same emblem that had appeared in all his visions. This was it. He closed his eyes, awash with silent relief.

When he opened his eyes again, the vision had vanished as if it had never been. All that was left was the fast-moving cloud of dust that denoted the rider's rapid westward progress. Straightaway, his mind tried to tell him that he had been seeing things, that he was so weary from his night-climb that he had dozed and dreamt as he sat, but his heart was pounding so hard that it seemed determined to gainsay the doubts. No consternation anywhere in the land implied that anyone else had seen the vision, but he trusted the insistence of his heart. He got to his feet in growing excitement.

He turned his eyes back northward, towards the mountains. Somewhere up there was the home he had been forced to leave behind. A home he might never see again. With his waking eyes he saw a cottage burning, the mountain-faces above lit red by the glare. He heard breaking glass and vengeful voices. He felt again the thud of hoof-beats as the pony carried the boy into the unknown. He closed his eyes to shut out the memories, and slowly, with the unclenching of his fists, they died away behind his eyelids. Turning his back on the pain-filled past, he opened his eyes again and looked west to the white-walled city.

If the rider of the vision was heading for Mariston then so would he. He would go to the capital and find him. Would there be a message or set of instructions? A guide to take him back, perhaps? After so long, the old man owed him that much at least. Pushing those thoughts aside, he set off down the steep slope in an eager shuffle.

The rider wore no obvious mark or emblem. She was dressed in black with silver edgings and there seemed to be strange devices or runes on her cloak that only showed as the light directly caught them. She wore a silver helm with great purple plumes flowing back from it and her visor was down so that her face was hidden. Her belt was studded with gems and from it hung both an ornate scabbard and a satchel, which both bore the symbol of a great six-pointed star with burning torches about it, and flaming runes conveying some strange motto. She was going at a mighty speed, the flagstones of the road sparking as her horse's shoes struck them. The road wound around the feet of a great hill which overlooked the city, before leading down to Mariston itself. As she rounded the hill the rider cast the token into the air, watching over her shoulder as the vision sprang out of it to fill the sky. That was all she had been bidden to do. Here, in this exact spot. She hoped the recipient was watching, or her master would be displeased. But she had other business too, so she left the enchantment to work itself and kept spurring on towards the city.

She rode at breakneck pace up the road. Heedless of the people who leapt out of her way, she galloped all the way to the great outer walls of the armist capital. Others like her had ridden the length and breadth of Ciroken and Ebinnin to every major city in every realm. They had gone to Kalator and Rohandur in the north; to the Silver City of elven Ithrill; to the halls of all the major Clan-lords in Aranar; to Paeyeir, the ancient citadel of the elves in Kalimar; to Carthak, the deep and forgotten citadel of the dwarves; and even to the extreme south where dwelt roving sun-darkened tribes. It had fallen to her to come to the capital city of Maristonia and deliver not one but two messages.

With one already delivered, she focused now on the other. Pulling up in a cloud of dust, she patted her steaming horse and caught her breath. The fabled walls towered above her, impossibly high. She looked up, up, up, craning her neck to look at the top of the gatehouse. The sentries at its top were almost out of sight. Made of stone hewn from the Carthaki Mountains, the portcullis had been fashioned in impenetrable steel by the elven-smiths of old. Vast oaken gates glowered across a long drawbridge which ran over the lake-like moat. Cut from the biggest trees, they were covered in carvings and bound by steel bands. They were the outward symbol of Mariston's might and wealth. Not as fair as the jewel-encrusted citadels of Kalimar, thought the rider, but stronger certainly. The first armist chieftains had done their work well: this was an unbreakable obstacle, behind which a few could defy all the hordes of the world.

She could have joined the queue pressing through a door within the great gates, but she had no time for such formalities. Instead, she gazed at the first parapet where the lowest sentries looked out from just above the gates. Their comrades at the top of the wall were scarcely within shouting range. She fixed her eyes on one of the sentries, and waited for the silent scrutiny to take effect. Soon the armist soldier began to look distinctly uncomfortable, and, searching around for the cause, his eyes alighted on the strange rider below, standing apart from the rest.

'Who are you?' he called down. 'Why have you come to the gates of Curillian, Lord of Maristonia?' The rider sat quite still for a moment, then lifted the visor of her helm. From beneath it, her pale elven face looked up. The sentry gaped down, blinking in surprise. She reached down to her satchel and took from it a roll of parchment. It was rolled about a gilt wooden frame, sealed and hung with a silver tassel. Then she allowed her clear voice to ring up.

'I bear a message for the king. It is for your king's eyes alone; will he receive it?' The words, soft yet commanding, drifted up to the sentry, who looked uncertain, more at the rider's outlandish garb and accent than at her simple words. Ordinary people in the queue and other sentries had heard the foreign voice and turned to look. The first sentry had gone to fetch a superior, who promptly came down and out of the gates with a detachment of soldiers.

'I am Captain of the Watch; I will read your message and judge whether it is worthy of His Majesty's attention.' The elf messenger looked coldly down at him, and then shot a volley of foreign words at him.

'*Ai-va, Curillian Haretholin, Ar i ce del i ce alan, valoreé egin ce Ciryád i Amagaïd.*' The captain's face fell. 'Fool, do you speak the tongue this message is written in? Do not waste my master's time, set wings to your feet and find someone with the wit to understand me, and whom I can trust to deliver my message to the hands of the king.' Unhappily, the captain went about obliging this request, while the onlookers slowly lost interest as the rider waited, still as a stone. At length, a larger squad of soldiers arrived, this time with a more senior-looking officer at their head. Waving his armists back, he walked out to meet the rider. His importance was proclaimed by the long black cloak he wore over his mail-coat, and by the red-plumed helm of gold enclosing his face. He walked like he owned the gateway.

'Hail, visitor from afar.' He laid a hand across his breast by way of salute. 'I am Lancoir, Knight of the Order of Thainen and Captain of the Royal Guard. I have the ear of the king. I will convey your message. Since I hear you are in haste, surrender the scroll to me, and I will take it to my king.' The elf inclined her head and extended her hand with the scroll. Yet before she relinquished it, she spoke a warning.

'My master laid great emphasis on the fact that only the intended recipient should read what is contained herein. Know that if any hands but the sovereign's open this wallet, they shall burn and wither before their eyes.' Lancoir held the other's eyes steadily as she spoke, though they were both fair and fell. 'I have no need to wait for a reply, if the king finds the message acceptable, he will seek out my master.' In the blink of an eye, the strange rider had turned her horse away and galloped back the way she had come.

Lancoir watched the receding rider for a few moments, then considered the package in his hands. When he realised his armists were watching him, he sent them scurrying back to their duties with a bark. He himself hastened to his horse in the gatehouse's stable. With his escort he rode swiftly through the streets of Mariston, over the bridges, under the gates of all the walls (for there were five walls, each with its own moat, each circular, getting progressively smaller) and so came to the innermost area of the city. Here, on a small armist-made island, stood the magnificent palace of the kings of Maristonia, the Carimir. It was built of white stone and marble. Its many towers, domes, golden roofs and crystal spires gave it a skyline which defied description. In the heart of the palace, the king resided in the tallest tower, and thither now was the Captain of the Royal Guard bound, treading familiar corridors. He ran into no obstructions, for all knew him and knew his status; instead, each guard he passed snapped to attention and saluted.

On his way he passed many disconsolate folk going the other way. Their number increased steadily, so that when he reached the corridor leading to the Royal Audience Chamber they filled the passageway, grumbling and shuffling away from the doors. On either side of this broad corridor were apertures inhabited by the effigies of past kings and their families, and from these apertures scarcely noticed Royal Guardsmen kept careful watch. Despite his haste, his eyes missed nothing, making sure they were properly alert. Now at last he was checked. The Announcer put a hand on his chest to intercept him. Without even looking up, he told him, 'His Majesty is no longer receiving supplicants. Wait until tomorrow.' He had not noticed the dozen Royal Guardsmen, who were arrayed in two squads either side of the gilt doors, snap to attention, and it was only when Lancoir boomed in a voice of inimitable authority that he looked up from his parchment.

'Tell His Majesty that Lancoir is here.' The guardsmen smiled as the Announcer nearly fell backwards in fright, scattering his documents. He made several apologies as he scurried around picking up his papers, and in the meantime two of the guardsmen heaved the doors inward. Without waiting to be 'Announced', the Captain of the Royal Guard, the most celebrated soldier in the realm, strode into the vast chamber. Filled with unimaginable riches, the Royal Audience Chamber was designed to accommodate thousands. And to overawe those thousands. Every last inch of wall was covered in tapestries, portraits and artistic friezes. The ceiling dripped with gold and crystal, and even the floor, either side of a single, red carpet, was covered in carvings telling a thousand stories of the Harolin dynasty's greatness. All the light came from the far end of the hall, where great stained-glass windows filled the wall. The hall ended in a great projecting bay, where the red carpet ended and the royal dais lay. The chamber, and indeed the whole tower, had been designed to face east so that light could glorify the morning Audiences. Now the multi-hued radiance flooded in and bathed the dais in great rays, with the effect that the thrones upon it, and their occupants, could barely be seen. Thus, the King of Maristonia, whenever beheld up close by his subjects, existed in a world of dazzling glory.

Even Lancoir, who was not easily intimidated, never failed to be impressed by the effect contrived by the Harolins and their architects. And even he could not see the persons on the dais. He kept approaching, but long before his eyes could penetrate the glittering scene, he was hailed.

'Lancoir, I thought it might be you. Come in. Welcome.' It was the noble voice of Queen Carmen, though he could still not see her.

'Your Majesty?'

'I'm by the windows, Lancoir, come.' At last he saw her, standing by the window, looking out over the palace gardens. She was so bathed with light, and her dress so brilliantly white, that she was all but invisible from beyond the dais. Her husband, however, was nowhere to be seen. Beautiful and erect as a portrait, she turned and smiled at him. Seeing her face, Lancoir fell to one knee and waited for invitation.

'Rise, Sir Lancoir, son of Lorumon, rise. You are looking for His Majesty, no doubt? He grew weary of proceedings and expelled the supplicants, along with the entire court, and retired up yonder staircase.'

'I have with me an urgent message for his attention, Your Majesty.'

'You are free to seek him out, faithful Lancoir. I hope your missive offers some relief from his present boredom.' Polite and gracious to a fault, the queen showed no interest in further conversation.

'By your leave, Your Majesty.' Lancoir turned away and the queen turned back to the window. The staircase she had indicated was concealed behind a great hearth in the centre of the northern wall, and it was expressly reserved for royal use and those given special royal permission. Lancoir was one of perhaps half a dozen people not related to the king by blood who even knew of its existence. Climbing it, he knew he was entering the private warren of Maristonia's sovereign, which meant that King Curillian could be in any of dozens of locations. Not fully familiar with this tower-top labyrinth, Lancoir knew he could be searching for a long time if his master did not wish to be found. Not in the Library. Not in the Reading Room. Not in the Viewing Hole, with its 360-degree panoramas of the city and its many telescopes. Similarly he checked off the Games Room, the Chapel, countless hidden passages and even the Royal Bedchamber and Bathchamber. At a loss, he stopped in the Library and called aloud.

'Your Majesty, it is Lancoir. Where are you to be found?'

Footsteps, distant yet close by, a turning of levers and a small section of bookcase pivoted into the air. A most unkingly figure, with rolled sleeves and begrimed face, peeped out of the new aperture, and greeted him cheerfully.

'Lancoir, no less – this is a pleasant surprise. Well, you've uncovered another secret refuge of mine, so you might as well come in. Come along, come along. It's no good standing on ceremony, you have to get your hands dirty to use some of these passages.' With that he vanished back into the hole. Immaculate as his office required, yet not personally fastidious, Lancoir followed him in and found himself having to stoop in a rough-hewn tunnel. Before long, he was forced to crawl in order to keep going, while his quincentennial king scampered along somewhere ahead with the nimbleness of a chimney sweep. Eventually he dropped down into a most curious chamber, lit both by braziers and small windows. Its walls contained countless inset shelves containing all manner of paraphernalia, presumably relevant to the vast war-gaming table which dominated the pit-like bottom of the room. King Curillian was already back amongst his cavalry squadrons and battalions, hard at play.

'Antruphan says this particular passageway will be finished in a week, and then connected to the others a few weeks after that,' the king informed his new guest while charging a knight-figurine forwards.

'Truly, Your Majesty's Master-mason is the envy of the Architects Guild, to receive so many royal commissions.'

'My dear Lancoir, he is one of those rare armists who combines great skill with great discretion. When the others could say as much, I might consider them. Anyway, how many times have I told you, drop the formalities.'

'As you will, sire.'

'Better, but as to relevance and directness, nothing beats Curillian.'

'Yes...Curillian.' The king showed a curious attachment to his name, thought Lancoir. Here was an armist who possessed a dozen glittering titles, and yet who preferred his ordinary baptismal name. For his part, very few people ever called him Lancoir without using the knightly Sir before it. Most just called him Sir. He could have been called anything and he wouldn't have cared, so long as people respected him. Yet he kept his thoughts to himself whilst standing bolt upright and gazing fixedly above his king's head. Curillian took a seat and regarded him carefully. As ever, Lancoir felt sure his thoughts were being guessed with uncanny perspicacity.

'You know, Lancoir, an armist values a name much more when he has been deprived of it. Curillian I was in my youth – Amazing Whiteness – an odd name, but my parents must have had their reasons. That name I was forced to relinquish, and I wandered as the Exile, Nadihoan, before being baptised in battle as Ruthion, the Red Warrior. Long and hard I had to fight to be allowed to come home and be Curillian again. I prize that name above all others, because it represents everything that I lost, and everything that I regained.

'But you, Lancoir. Enduring Silver. Your loyalty and steadfastness are as true as silver, and as enduring as the purest silver that the elves say fell from the stars. Silver runs through your name and your reputation, just as it does for King Lancearon of Ithrill, the Silver Helm.'

'So I have been told,' said Lancoir, unconvinced. Curillian continued, unperturbed.

'Lancoir, hear me in this. Names, like salvation, are from Prélan Himself. And like salvation, which we must receive with faith, names must be grasped, taken to heart, and lived out.' He paused, still pondering his visitor. 'What do you think?'

'I think,' began Lancoir before hesitating, 'I think that you think too much about such things.' Curillian laughed.

'Well, that's true,' said he. 'I have plenty of time for thinking. Too much. But come, there are plenty with whom you could better discuss nomenclature in the University; why have you come?'

'I have a message to deliver, sire, a very strange message.' The king smiled as the old habit of deference crept back in unnoticed. 'It bears the mark of no lord or institution that I recognise. Wherever it has come from, it's beyond the bounds of my knowledge.' Curillian heard the unease in his captain's voice and his interest was piqued. 'Will you receive it here?' Curillian thought a moment.

'No, since you have disturbed my game, I will receive it in my Bedchamber...and let Carmen be present. Come.'

The king led the way back through the tunnel and through the labyrinth of apartments to his Bedchamber. The king's actual sleeping chamber was still further within, but this opulent outer chamber was where the most important of messengers were received. The king's ceremonial robes – gorgeous white patterned silk, edged with facings of crimson velvet – still hung where they had been discarded after the supplicants had been ejected. Preferring to stay in his tunnel-grimed shirt and trousers, Curillian settled himself in a seat and studied the message while Lancoir went to find the queen. The message was contained within a leather pouch, covered with runes and designs of the most outlandish sort. He was still scrutinising it when the queen entered with Lancoir in tow. Curillian was just about to jump up and greet his wife, but she moved swiftly to him, kissing his forehead and encouraging him to remain seated. Then she took another of the seats. Both then looked at Lancoir. Curillian tossed him the pouch.

'Do the honours old friend.' He raised an eyebrow when Lancoir, normally so efficient and unflappable, hesitated, looking worried.

'Sire, the message was expressly for your eyes only...on pain of... maiming.' Concerned and intrigued in equal measure, the king leaned forward and took the pouch back again. 'Well, if my enemies have hatched some plot, it's been a long time in coming...' Not without a little trepidation of his own, he untied the thongs knotting it shut. No sooner had the knot come undone than the message sprang out of the king's hand as if it had a life of its own. Lancoir stepped backwards, hand flying to his sword-hilt, and Carmen rose in alarm, but Curillian remained sitting, hunched forward in fascination. Suspended in mid-air of its own accord, the unfurled message looked just like an ordinary letter, but then it started glowing at the edges, as if being held too close to a candle. All of a sudden, it burst into a kaleidoscopic mirage of colours and forms. These filled the air for a fleeting second before suddenly contracting and coalescing like an explosion reversed. A small incandescent orb was all that remained, but slowly it grew, until a face could be discerned in its midst. On first glance the face seemed to belong to a tired old man, but then a mantle of snowy hair, like a garment of wisdom, and grey eyes full of memory and knowledge, became apparent. The face spoke, and its voice was invested with age-old authority.

Kulothiel, Keeper of Oron Amular, and Head of the League of Wizardry, to Curillian son of Mirkan son of Arimaya, King of Maristonia, greetings in Prélan's name. You must excuse the theatrics, but in this age of suspicion and doubt, I deemed it necessary to preface what is to follow with a small token of its authenticity. The world is changing, and my place in it is fast diminishing, but I find that my office has one duty yet to discharge for the benefit of the Free Peoples. Even as a third stormcloud gathers in the North, I invite you to a Tournament here in Oron Amular. Upon the first full moon of summer, many are invited to gather here. The prize for which you shall compete is an heirloom of Power Unimaginable. Other rewards you may also find. I trust I do not misjudge in appealing to your restless talents. Prélan's speed.

The mellifluous voice ceased and the whole vision faded. The room was recalled to normality from the stuff of dreams. As if a string had been cut, the letter dropped to the floor. Gingerly, Lancoir picked up the object. The leather packaging remained as it had looked before, but the page within was blank. He proffered it to his sovereign, who still sat hunched forward with the same expression of rapt fascination.

Curillian did not appear to heed his captain, but instead muttered to himself.

'He speaks as if he knew me…' Recovering from the intensity of the spectacle, Queen Carmen spoke to her husband.

'All those times we heard his name, but never once did either of us meet him. Why does he address himself to you now?' Her eyes were sad but understanding when she watched the transformation in her beloved. The enchantment was replaced by boisterous excitement, as if it had been a crumbling sluice-gate washed away by a sudden spate. Curillian repeated the two words to himself three times, each time getting more voluble.

'Oron Amular…Oron Amular…ORON AMULAR…' With the last utterance he leapt to his feet, the light of adventure in his eyes. 'I am called…to Oron Amular? What a prospect Prélan sends me in His mercy to stave off senile dotage for a few more years. All these years I thought He'd forgotten me, but now, now at last a new game's afoot.'

'My darling,' his wife said soothingly, 'try not to get too carried away just yet. None now know how to find Oron Amular, and even if they did, it would be a long way away, and beyond many dangers.'

'Beyond many rivers and mountains, I've no doubt. Someone, I'm sure, can be found to lead me thither. Let me see now, how to get there, and who to take…' The king would have gone on apace with his plans had not the Captain of his Royal Guard interrupted.

'But Your Majesties…' They both turned to look at him. 'You speak as if this message is genuine, as if Oron Amular really exists…' Curillian smiled at him.

'Lancoir the Unpersuadable! Verily, even if a trickster took in every wise armist in the realm, still you would be unconvinced. Has it not brought you to where you are – so high in my service – along with your martial valour and unstained personal honour? Yet a cynical armist may become so cynical in filtering all the counterfeits aimed at a king that he may miss the real thing. Oron Amular does exist, though the world may have forgotten it. Carmen and I met several of the protégés of Kulothiel in Silverdom, and I fought alongside them in the Second War of Kurundar. Like most others, I do not understand High Magic, or Black Magic, but I've seen enough of both with my own eyes to be convinced that it does indeed exist beneath the sun. Is what we've just seen not proof of that? And yet we've heard nor seen nothing of it for hundreds of years…until now. My dear Lancoir, can't you see how exciting this is?'

'I can see how dangerous it is, sire,' Lancoir responded staunchly. 'The southern frontier is quiet, but far from stable. There is much to be done in your own realm. What if the barbarians should rise up again when you have gone to foreign parts?'

'General Otaken and the Constable of the South-fold can handle anything the Alanai can throw at them, just as their predecessors have done for generations uncounted. The southern front is as quiet as I have ever known it, and all else is quieter still. Can you *not* see? This is just what I have been waiting for.' Lancoir looked unhappy, but refrained from arguing further. Curillian turned to his queen. 'Beloved, will you excuse us?' Carmen nodded resignedly. Curillian sprang towards the door. 'Come, Lancoir,' he beckoned. 'We have many preparations to make.' Queen Carmen's voice checked him just as he reached the door.

'If you must go out, dear,' she said, 'at least put on a clean shirt and coat.' Curillian looked down at his grimy attire and smiled. To Lancoir's startled discomfort, he stripped his dirty shirt off right there and then. A forest of scars from old battles was plain to see, but the muscles were those of a much younger armist. He donned a new shirt, seized his white and gold brocade coat, bowed to his wife, and was gone.

He stormed along the corridor at a great pace, pulling on his coat and tidying his hair as he went. Lancoir, struggling to keep up, came up alongside. Never breaking stride around all the corners and down all the steps of his chambers, Curillian rattled off instructions to the Captain of his Guard.

'Lancoir, I want you to assemble a cohort of the Royal Guard. Which is the unit with that new commander?'

'Surumo?'

'Yes, he impressed me when we met.'

'Third Cohort, sire. Piron is his second-in-command.'

'Curillian, Lancoir, not sire. The Third? Yes, they'll do. Have them assembled and ready to ride in two days. They must have baggage and provisions for a month on the road. I want messages sent on ahead by the quickest errand-riders to summon the finest trackers and pathfinders of the Eastern Army. They will rendezvous with us at Arket two weeks from now. I myself am going to the Royal Library, where I will be investigating Oron Amular for the rest of the day. Have Arton, General Gannodin and My Lord High Chancellor ready to meet me in my State-room at sundown tonight...Oh, and make sure Téthan is there, too.'

'As you command, sire.'

Curillian stopped. They had now reached the public part of the palace and were standing at the top of the staircase which led down into the grand Entrance Hall. Here they parted ways, but Curillian remonstrated with his captain first.

'Lancoir?'

'Sire?'

'If you address me as 'sire' one more time, you won't accompany me to Oron Amular.' The king smiled when he saw the surprise register in Lancoir's face: clearly he had not presumed upon this honour.

'Yes...Curillian...' he said at length. Curillian clapped him on the shoulder.

'Good armist.'

'Are you telling me you really have no idea whatsoever?' Curillian demanded. The old scholar straightened up, creaking as he did so, and sneezed from all the dust covering the ancient tome in front of him. He looked apologetically at his king.

'My profound apologies, sire, but this is the oldest volume we have. Our records only go back so far. I'm afraid certain sections of the archives were rather badly neglected when...when Your Majesty was abroad for so long.' Curillian impatiently waved him past the awkward allusion and pressed him further. 'The section on Kalimar was among them. One or two of the older monasteries might have histories going back further, but even if they did...well...exact directions wouldn't often have been written down. The League was, by all accounts, very secretive about such things. I doubt whether even many of the works in Kalimar itself would shed more light on the matter. The League seems to have been defunct for almost five hundred years, and before that it had been getting increasingly more mysterious for centuries.'

Curillian sighed with frustration at the old scholar's lisping, wheezy ruminations. The Royal Library was located in the westernmost of the palace's three towers and took up several whole floors. Shunning the open way from his own apartments in the central tower in preference for the secret passages which he loved, Curillian had moved from the Writing Room of his Secretariat to the Royal Library without being seen by anyone. Now, after two hours of trawling through old parchments and manuscripts with old Comangen, he sat on a bench amid the stacks, irritated and grouchy. Old Comangen, practically blind and rheumatic, was the acknowledged expert amongst the royal archivists on Kalimar – the ancient elvish realm – and all things elvish. If anyone would know the whereabouts of Oron Amular, it would be him. But now, after enduring the slow unravelling of his long erudition, it appeared that even Comangen knew little more than his colleagues, some of whom had barely heard of the League of Wizardry. A thousand and a half years ago, or so it was said, the League had had its own resident ambassador at the court of the Maristonian king, but now the lore of Oron Amular in the armist realm had shrivelled to a sad level of ignorance. The thickness of dust covering all the elven manuscripts testified to the dwindling interest in that subject. Making one last effort, Curillian appealed to one of the newly dusted maps of Kalimar.

'Can you at least indicate a rough location?'

'Perhaps, sire,' mumbled Comangen, wiping his nose and leaning in close to the new resource. He hummed and muttered to himself for a while. 'Hmmm, yes, well, I think I could safely say it lies somewhere in this area.' Curillian inspected the chosen point on the map. Comangen's finger was tracing an infuriatingly wide circle in western Kalimar.

'But that's an area that covers most of the Black Mountains, and a lot of Dorzand and northern Kalimar with it! I could have an entire legion of trackers scouring such an area for months and still not find every mountain!' He put his fingers to his forehead in exasperation, trying to block out the sound of Comangen's breathing. 'Oh, it's hopeless,' he said after a while. Then, 'Or maybe I have a better idea...' He got up and made to leave, but before doing so, he rounded on the archivist. 'This archive's a disgrace, Comangen. When I'm back, I'll have words with the Head Librarian. You and he had better get it back into some sort of shape or I'll transfer you both to stable duty.'

Fortunately for the Head Librarian, he was not to be found when Curillian came back to the library's entrance. Returning by the secret passages to the Writing Room of his Secretariat, he summoned a clerk to him.

'Have a runner go to the Kalimari Embassy. If the ambassador is home, I want to see him in the Royal Audience Chamber an hour before dusk.'

The elf standing next to him was tall and saturnine. Together they stood watching the late afternoon through the windows of the Royal Audience Chamber. Shadows were fast growing in the east-facing room.

'I was delighted to find that Your Eminence could join me at such short notice,' Curillian told his guest. The ambassador of Kalimar never took his eyes from the window.

'Long has it been since I have been summoned so urgently. I am honoured by your eagerness, Your Majesty.' Curillian smiled inwardly. Despite the tedious official cordiality of diplomatic parlance, he knew as well as the ambassador that neither of them was happy at the hasty manner of this meeting. The representative of the oldest nation in the world did not take kindly to being summoned on a whim, and Curillian could practically smell the resentment rising off him like steam from a spent horse. Just as aloof as the Hendarian Ambassador, this misanthropic elf was even more reclusive.

'I've asked you here to have your help in finding Oron Amular.' Curillian cut straight to it, but the elf maintained his silent scrutiny of the view. Curillian studied him, guessing that the considered non-reaction was a likely indication that Kalimar knew all about

Kulothiel's invitations. Eventually, unwavering examination induced the ambassador to turn and face him, looking down gravely at the armist king. 'Come,' said Curillian, 'you know the way, do you not?' The ghost of a smile hovered on the ambassador's lips.

'Your Majesty, it is with great regret that I cannot speak to you with candour on this matter.'

'Perhaps one of your kindred might be more forthcoming if I were to conduct enquiries in Alkala? Lovely part of the world, and I do so love to edge across the border every now and then…' The suggestion had barely left Curillian's lips when another evasion was proffered.

'I fear there is no one in Alkala, or anywhere along the Armist Road, who would be able to satisfactorily answer such an enquiry, much as they would like to assist Your Majesty.' Curillian sighed extravagantly.

'It seems that the obscurity of the Mountain of High Magic is not so much down to forgetfulness as to intentional design. Tell me, Eminence, what would happen if a large and inquisitive delegation were to cross the border with the peaceful intention of finding said mountain?' There was the ghost of another, entirely unamused smile.

'His Immortal Majesty, King Lithan, son of Avallonë, son of Avalar, would take a very dim view indeed of such an errand.' Curillian stepped away and began to pace a tight circle nearby. Soon he stopped and regarded the ambassador again.

'You will forgive me, Eminence, but I grow weary of these circuitous niceties. Talk plainly to me. Has Kulothiel dispatched invites to a tournament, or has he not?' Curillian read in the other's eyes exactly what he wanted to.

'Whether or not there is a tournament is for the invitee alone to know. Word has reached me, however, that I am not to extend any insight or assistance to anyone who might ask about Oron Amular.'

'No doubt similar instructions have reached your esteemed colleagues in Hamid, Rohandur and Kalator? Let us just suppose, for a moment, that Your Eminence knew about such a tournament as this – how would you expect the entrants to participate if they cannot even find the venue?'

'It is all part of the test.'

Five people were waiting for Curillian in his State-room. Smaller and more intimate than the Royal Audience Chamber, it was nevertheless just as grand. Being on the western side of the central tower of the palace, it basked now in the dying rays of the sun. Languid red-golden light sifted through the opulent chamber. The first to greet him was the small boy who came flying at him.

'Father!' Fondness suffused Curillian as his son Téthan ran up and hugged him. Picking up the little bundle of energy, he walked further into the room, nodding in acknowledgement to the others present as he did so. He set the boy down by his favourite chair and kissed the top of his head. Settling back into his seat, he turned his attention to those waiting upon him: a duke, a palace official and a soldier. Cardanor, Duke of Arton, was the seniormost noblearmist in the realm, not related to the king by blood, but whom Curillian thought of as a younger brother. Ophryior, the Lord High Chancellor, was Curillian's most important minister, responsible for both the Royal Treasury and Secretariat. Gorgeously apparelled in robes of state, he embodied the grandeur and majesty of the realm far more often than did his more casual sovereign. Gannodin, a grizzled old warrior, was the general in command of the Ist Legion, the prestigious elite unit of the Maristonian Army which formed part of the garrison of

Mariston. And then there was Lancoir, faithful and vigilant as ever, standing quietly in a dark corner.

'Arton,' Curillian beckoned the young duke closer. 'In two days I will be leaving the capital on a discreet and private venture. I want you to head up things here while I'm gone. Are you up to it?'

'Of course, Curillian.' The king smiled.

'Good armist, I knew you would be. Ophryior here will help you in the running of things, won't you Ophryior?' The Lord High Chancellor bowed immaculately, his face a mask of uncompromising efficiency. Curillian turned to the general.

'Gannodin, can the Eastern Army spare a legion?' The general grunted in what could loosely be interpreted as an affirmative response. Curillian carried on seamlessly. 'Good, Horuistan's 15th should do – they're at Arket, yes? Prepare immediate open orders for them to conduct exercises in The Bowl, and prepare closed orders also, to let Horuistan know to expect me within two weeks.' Gannodin grunted again, but this time he followed it up with a short, barked question.

'You expecting trouble, sire?'

'It's not impossible. My guess is that this tournament may attract unwanted attention from those not invited, and I'd like some seasoned troops nearby, just in case.'

'And if anyone asks why a whole legion is exercising in the East-fold…?'

'Tell them we've heard rumours that the harracks are causing trouble.' Next it was Cardanor who leaned in with a question.

'Curillian, Lancoir has told us the basic details, but won't you tell us more? What is this tournament? Can you even find a way there?' Curillian reflected a moment, palms flat against each other.

'Whatever it is, Kulothiel must have good reason for breaking his centuries-long silence. The Hendarians tell us there's trouble in the north again, and it wouldn't surprise me if there's a connection. Some last throw of the League of Wizardry, who knows?'

'But can you find the Mountain?' the duke pressed him. 'I thought no one knew where it was.'

'Well, Comangen knows even less than the little I thought he did, and the maps are worse. The Kalimari ambassador was hardly forthcoming – my guess is Kulothiel's told the elves not to give anyone help that would be unfair. King Lithan wouldn't help, even if he wanted to, and I've got no intention of forcing his hand. He may even be competing himself. That leaves me with a couple of options, but you can let me and Lancoir worry about that.' The Captain of the Royal Guard pricked his ears to an extra level of alertness. 'Is my cohort making ready, Lancoir?'

'They are indeed…Curillian.' The king smiled, doubly satisfied.

'Good.' He pulled his son close. 'Now listen to me, Téthan, son, I'm going to be away for a short while.'

'Like when you were smashing the barbarians?' the boy piped up eagerly.

'Yes, just like then, only maybe not so long this time. I'm glad to see your history lessons are sticking.' Téthan had not even been born when Curillian had fought his latest campaign against the troublesome tribes on his southern border. 'But while I'm away, Uncle Arton here will look after you, and teach you lots of interesting things.'

'More interesting than old Gaeon?'

'Yes, even more interesting than your tutor. And,' he leaned in close, 'even more fun,' he promised in a conspiratorial whisper. Téthan beamed with pleasure. 'But remember,' Curillian warned his son, 'you must always obey your mother.' Téthan nodded. 'Now off you go with Uncle Arton, he'll take you back to your mother.' Duke and prince walked out by a side-door, both equally happy in each other's company.

Curillian stood up. 'Well, gentlemen, I think we're done. I bid you all a pleasant night.' His good wishes were returned elegantly by Ophryior, and rather less elegantly by Gannodin. After them Lancoir took his leave, and Curillian departed to be with his wife.

Carmen was already in bed, but not asleep. She sat up, waiting for him. She watched him as he slowly took off his clothes. With an effort, she kept her mind on other things.

'Did your meetings go as you hoped?'

'Well… yes and no,' he answered, casting aside the last garments. 'Everything has been set in order here with Arton and Ophryior, but the ambassador was less than helpful.' He settled in next to her under the bedclothes.

'How is Melnova?' One of the kingdom's greatest epic poets lay unread in the queen's hand; she had quite forgotten she was holding it.

'What? Oh, fine…fine.' Curillian leaned in and gave his wife a kiss on the cheek.

'She has quite a way with words, doesn't she?' he observed, then, changing subject abruptly. 'Téthan should get on well with Arton – they are a good influence on each other. Ophryior will hold the fort administratively, and the important matters can wait till I get…are you all right, sweetness? You seem preoccupied…' Curillian could tell she hadn't taken on board what he'd said, and yet she appeared unwilling to share what was on her mind. He shifted on to his side to attend to his bed-side lamp and stopped short, feeling the hands on his back. Her fingers traced the old scars, and he lay still, allowing her hands to move freely.

'Must you go?' The pent up question slipped out at last. Curillian gazed into the lamp's flame for a few moments before responding.

'Yes.' The pause was pregnant.

'But why? You've fought your battles, earned your stripes, lived your adventures. Isn't now the time to rest and enjoy the life we've worked so hard for?' He rolled back over, so as to face her.

'Carmen, I don't want to stop having adventures until I die. I was born to it, raised and confirmed in crisis, and ever after had my heart fixed on it, on the challenge, the excitement. Have you forgotten it, the headiness of the early days? It was like strong wine…'

'I remember. We came together in unusual circumstances, and our deeds against the Usurper are rightly glorious in the eyes of your people, but it was a long time ago. Things are different now. I find I no longer have the appetite for the breakneck life. Alas, I am not so evergreen as you, though much grace has been given me, sailor's daughter. I married the dashing prince, and now I want to grow old in contentment with the venerable king.' She snuggled up close to him, kissing his neck. 'Can you not be content with that?' Curillian smiled wryly.

'Venerable, am I? That makes me sound nearly six hundred.' She nuzzled him.

'You *are* over five hundred.'

He pulled away slightly. 'And yet I still feel two hundred. My hands and feet are restless, my mind is restless. I yearn for more…'

'You are *King*, lord of a wide realm and father of a free people. What more is there?'

'*Power Unimaginable*.' He breathed the response so lightly that she barely caught it. A look of concern came into her face.

'Do not let the old wizard tempt you. His day is over. You have no need of whatever relic or toy he cares to hold out.'

'And yet it remains for every armist to challenge the bounds of the ordinary, be he serf or sovereign. Do not ask me to deny my soul.' She saw the light in his eyes, the fire that burned from a depth she could not reach, and knew her words were in vain.

'I do not ask it. But your soul is not your own – it belongs to Prélan – and He has given you duties, to your wife, to your son, to your people.'

He fixed her with a challenging look. 'Carmen, if you do not want me to go, say so and have done.' She regarded him sadly.

'Curillian, most precious love, I do not begrudge you your freedom or wish to deny your dreams. Your heart will lead you where it will, as it always has. How many rulers and powers have sought to constrain your heart and failed? Yet I am here to council you, to share my heart with you, and my heart warns me. You will over-reach yourself in this.' The protest died on his lips and he listened gravely, knowing the time-honoured wisdom of his wife. 'You are not talking about a pleasure cruise along the Mastred, or a hunt in Tol Verenen, or even a campaign against the Alanai. You propose to seek out the hidden Mountain and compete in ancient halls of sorcery. You will meddle with the policies and devices of mage-lords when you don't even know where to find them? Beware, my love, lest you fail at too stern a test. I fear that you might spoil the honourable autumn of your life, even at the last. Stay.' *And yet I know, in spite of all my words, you will still go.*

In the quiet early summer morning, Curillian sought out his escort. Soft golden light filtered down on the gardens and smooth stone walls; birds sang sweetly, and many fair waters trickled in a peaceful music of their own. The world seemed good. And yet his heart was heavy from the conflict within. His feet traversing well-known and beloved paths, he made his way to the stable-yard of the palace garrison. Distinct from the much larger stables in the Royal Square outside the palace, this smaller abode was home to the steeds of the Royal Guards who lived in ceaseless vigil about their sovereign. A full *militar* – 600 warriors – were thus stationed in the Carimir, the Palace of Carinen, five cohorts of 120 each who were the personal bodyguard of the king, elite warriors all. Separate to this, two legions were garrisoned in the city itself, and one of these – Gannodin's Ist Legion, the seniormost unit of the Maristonian Army, occupied four barracks all around the perimeter of the Royal Zone, the moated island at the heart of the city. In the event of trouble, the legion's 12,000 troops could surround the palace in a matter of minutes and thwart any enemy.

When Curillian came to the stables, he found everything virtually ready. The armists of the Third Cohort were all there, either standing patiently by their horses, or hurrying to stow the last of their baggage. Curillian knew they would have been up since before dawn, meaning that their weapons were all honed and their scabbards oiled; their clothing and provisions for the journey were already packed in neat bundles before and behind their saddles; their farewells to loved ones had been made and their instructions for the first day given. Surumo, the commander of the cohort, strode over.

'Morning Commander,' Curillian greeted him. 'Everything ready?' The question was merely polite, and quite unnecessary.

Surumo had overseen the whole operation. As soon as he had been given orders from Lancoir two days before, he would have had his troops focused on this moment. Last minute training, procurement of special equipment, all had been seen to.

'Yes sir, all ready. The lads are just waiting for your word, sir.' The guards all about were looking at their king in full readiness; affection, pride and excitement in their eyes. Curillian took a moment to take in their fondness. It filled his heart with glowing satisfaction and eased his doubts. Lancoir walked up, leading two horses. His own, kitted out like those of the cohort, bore no distinction, but the king's horse, Theamace, was altogether a more noble beast. Bred from among the long-lived horses of Aranar, which were of elven pedigree, he had been a faithful companion of Curillian's through many years and adventures. His saddle and bridle were finer than the other mounts, but Curillian had given specific instructions that the grandest tackle should be omitted. Likewise, the guards had exchanged their gleaming plated armour for chainmail and the muted garb of rangers, both less conspicuous and more practical. This would be a testing venture, treading unknown paths in the wild, but even on the easier roads at the outset Curillian wanted his riding to be discreet. While they retained the two-handed swords of which they were so proud, they now also carried bows, quivers, throwing axes and hunting knives, which were less usual weapons for them.

Curillian's pride from surveying the fine soldiery around him had turned into an odd sense of foreboding, his mind focusing on peculiar small details. The rich carvings on the stable-doors, the hop-skip of a crow in the rafters, the lucky coin poking from behind the ear of a guardsman. As soon as he became aware of this, he shrugged it off by propelling himself into the saddle, prompting his escort to do likewise. As was his long-time habit, he personally checked his own baggage and weapons, even though Lancoir would have been minutely scrupulous in doing so beforehand. His left hand was immediately drawn to the hilt of his sword, quite helpless against the magnificent weapon's magnetism. Something in the touch of it electrified him. The smouldering embers of adventure in his heart ignited into sudden flame. In a burst of energy, he spurred Theamace out into the courtyard, where the lofty towers of the palace soared up above him. The Third Cohort surged into the morning light, the clatter of their hooves reverberating. Outside, two other cohorts were drawn up in formal dress, flanking the path to the palace entrance as an honour-guard. Many intrigued servants were watching furtively, but the only intended audience stood at a balcony in one of the towers above.

Queen Carmen looked on demurely, her calm demeanour quite concealing the inner turmoil from her companions. With her were ladies-in-waiting, Lord High Chancellor Ophryior, Duke Cardanor of Arton, several officers of the Royal Guards, and her little son, Téthan. This royal party watched as the king led his knights in dismounting and kneeling beside their horses.

Before joining his followers on their knees, Curillian unsheathed the Sword of Maristonia, *Falakinde*. Forged by elf-lord Torlas of Camelar for his grandfather Arimaya over fifteen hundred years ago, it was *the* weapon of the kings of Maristonia. Even more so than the great walls of Mariston, it was the symbol of their formidable strength and justice. Blessed with spells during the forging, the fear it engendered smote all the harder, and the gleam of its metal shone all the brighter. It was a blade of destiny, potent and compelling. Holding it aloft to glimmer in the rays of the sun, Curillian turned a slow circle, displaying it to all present. Only then did he kneel, holding it point down and gripping the crosspiece with both hands. He bowed his head. The prayer he uttered could not be heard above, only by his guards.

'Prélan, Lord of Heaven and Father of the Faithful, hear this prayer and be with us now. Bless this riding, and go forth with us to victory. Guide us and protect us on whichever paths we tread. Give us the strength to conduct ourselves with honour and justice, as befits Your warriors. Give us wisdom, that we might fight only the good fight. Grant that whatever success we find redound to the Glory of Your Name and the increase of Your Kingdom among us. In Your holy name, Amen.'

He should have got up then, but he did not, could not. His guards waited impatiently behind him. As soon as he had raised his eyes, he saw the emissary of Prélan, white-clad and glowing, come and stand before him. Angelic hands were clasped around his, still holding the sword. He heard the voice swirling around his head like an orchestrated storm of wind.

The Lord is with you, mighty warrior. Go in the strength that you have. Protect him, for he is needed at the Mountain. And whatever prize you win, be ready to relinquish.

Curillian choked and shook, overcome by the encounter. Lancoir was poised ready to spring like a cat to his assistance, but the king managed to get to his feet unaided. He looked unsteady at first, but strength grew with every step. When he raised the sword again, its brightness was redoubled as if it had sapped the morning light around it for its own brilliance. Raising their eyes, the awed guards saw the light of heaven in their king's eyes, a look which had inspired so many of his followers before, but which none of them had ever seen. Were the tales really true, then? Was he really the chosen warrior of Prélan? Was he really invincible? No enemy had ever withstood him, they had been told, and now they believed.

Curillian leapt again into the saddle, even more invigorated than before, and Theamace reared high, as if sensing and sharing his master's joy. Hilt first, he saluted his son. Sword sheathed, he blew a kiss to his wife. She in turn held out a hand of farewell and blessing, and Téthan waved enthusiastically.

In a flash of speed Curillian turned and led his cavalcade in a whirl from the palace. Riding down the paved slope and under the tower-flanked gatehouse, they emerged into the Royal Square. Normally a royal exit would have been in a measured pace and accompanied by much ceremony and attention, but now they cantered across the plaza and did not slow down until they had crossed the south-eastern bridge into the Third Zone. They trotted briskly, not wishing to arouse too much attention.

The Royal Zone was the innermost sanctum of the city, encircled by three others, the Third, the Second and the Outer, each one wider than the one before. Of the three great gates out of the city, Curillian had chosen to exit by the southern one, for it was the least busy, and to get to it one rode through the quietest segment of the city. To use the North Gate, or the East Gate, where the messenger had met Lancoir, would have been to meet half the city along the way and fight through enormous crowds of merchants and farmers, drovers and carters, soldiers and foreign visitors. Even so, as they went, many people heard the rumour of their passing and flocked to line the streets where they rode.

Most petitioners would have been duped by the king's evasive route, but not this one. His was a special petition, an urgent petition, and it had to be today. His task could not be delayed, nor his offer made again once the opportunity was missed. Unfamiliar though he was with the city, especially this part of it, some guiding force greater than the will of Curillian brought his feet to the right place. Hurrying at unaccustomed speed, he arrived in the nick of time, exploding out of the side street onto the main thoroughfare in a red blur. The king's horse had only just enough time to rear to a sudden halt without smearing him into the road. The onlookers gasped. The spectacle of the great horse rearing over him was terrifying, and he cowered back onto the road, thinking at any moment that he would be trampled to death. Yet no sooner had the initial terror of the lead horse diminished than a second horse advanced up. A grim rider, hugely tall and menacing on his big steed, rode down on him, sending him scampering back along the road. A sword was unsheathed, but as it swung round into an attacking position, a voice of command rang out.

'Leave him be, Lancoir.' The rider of the first horse was on foot now and level with the other rider, who stopped advancing, but still stood high in his stirrups, a hovering, bullish menace. The dismounted rider walked ahead of the horses and confronted the armist whom he had nearly crushed. The newcomer now saw that, unlike the other mounted armists, this armist's hood had fallen down in the near miss and a circlet of silver with a blue sapphire at its front was evident upon his head. He had not been led wrong: this was the royal riding.

'My friend,' said the king, 'whatever your haste, I hope it was worth nearly being killed for.' The younger armist could only just manage to speak in response, the shock still causing his heart to pound and his breath to come in frantic gasps.

'Lord King, I came to offer you my service.' At the mention of that title, a buzz went through the onlookers; they had noticed the jewel and circlet too, but now their suspicions were confirmed: the king was here. The king's captain, who had seemed intent on trampling him, spat his derision.

'You?! What service could a beggar like you offer us?' The newcomer became keenly aware of his age-stained red and brown garments. He did indeed feel quite the beggar, but he was committed now; he might as well see it through. If the king was not amenable, then he had already done enough to merit the royal dungeons.

'I know where you are going. I'm going to the same place. I can help you.' Suspicion and wariness immediately came into the king's bemused face, but soon they were joined by a strange expression which the newcomer couldn't identify. They made a strange and vivid pair – the coroneted and mail-clad rider in rich green and black, and the dusty beggar in faded red – and Curillian suddenly became aware of the growing number of people watching, well within earshot. He strode resolutely towards his accoster; close enough so that only he could hear the next words.

'Where am I going?' The young armist now realised the need for discretion, despite having played the key role in its being thrown to the winds. He matched the king's low tone.

'Oron Amular, to the Mountain of High Magic. I can help you…I've been there.' Wonder and surprise showed in the king's face, but he mastered them within moments.

'Come then, and we shall see if your claim is true. Woe betide you, though, if you have spoken falsely.' He turned and beckoned to another senior-looking rider. 'Commander, a spare horse for this armist; he comes with us.' In startling speed, a horse with an empty saddle was brought up and the king remounted, ignoring the disapproving look of the knight beside him. In a trice, the whole cavalcade moved off again. They left behind them a bewildered crowd of city-dwellers rubbing their eyes and rummaging in their ears, wondering if they had really seen and heard what they thought they had.

The King's Cohort, though, was long gone. They slowed just enough for the lead riders to go on ahead and arrange clear passage at the South Gate. The guards at the gate opened wide the passage and cleared the crowds aside, so Curillian and his party of 123 were able to sweep through without so much as breaking pace. In a blur of green and brown they left the city behind and entered the townlands beyond. Now they spurred into a full gallop and were flying eastward. A tournament beckoned them.

II
Reflections

THEY rode hard all day until dusk was falling about them, and then Curillian called a halt. Long shadows were falling across the plains of central Maristonia. They bivouacked in a small copse beside the road. The armists of the Royal Cohort busied themselves erecting tents, setting pickets and cooking an evening meal. The young armist tagging along was extremely glad of the halt. Unused to riding, he was chafed raw and his muscles were burning. He burned, too, from the shame of the jeers and smirks of the skilled riders about him all day as they watched his efforts to keep up the pace and remain in his saddle. Now that they had stopped, he was ignored by them whilst the hustle and bustle went on all around him. Feeling suddenly at a loss, he took himself off to a quiet corner away from the rest and sat down against a tree, trying to get comfortable. He had no desire to join the rough camaraderie of the guards, which was quite incomprehensible to him. Try as he might, though, he could not relax. He discovered the reason why when he caught the hostile glare of the captain, the rider who had nearly trampled him. The hard-faced armist was staring at him with undisguised hostility. He felt the force of the gaze like an over-hot fire too close for comfort. Closing his eyes, he did his best to ignore it. When he opened them again he saw that a guardsman had distracted the captain, allowing him some respite. This was going to be a long journey.

The soldiers gradually formed into small groups around dozens of small campfires. They talked and jested over bowls of steaming broth, and the trees rang with their voices. Roujeark watched on, stomach rumbling. He gave up waiting for food to be offered to him and took a biscuit from his pouch to nibble. He was not unused to meagre fare, having trodden many lonely paths far from inns or markets. It had been a long day though, and the stale morsel did nothing to sate his appetite. So he was grateful when a shadow loomed over him. It was one of the soldiers, a duty cook, and the armist wordlessly plonked a bowl of broth into his lap. He ate the meal, whose main virtue was that it was hot, and felt a grudging thankfulness. As he blew on a spoonful of scalding liquid he became aware of the king picking his way amongst the circles of troops, conversing and joking with them. He was surprised when the monarch kept going and came to stand over him. The king looked down, regarding him silently. He seemed to be scrutinising him for some answer.

'We should talk,' he said at last. Silence fell amongst the guards nearby, who listened in until an officer snapped at them to be about their business. As they dispersed, the king beckoned for his new acquaintance to follow him. Picking up a flaming brand from one of the fires, he led him off into the trees away from the main camp. The ever-vigilant captain made to follow them, but Curillian waved him away. He sat them down between two pine trunks, and thrust the brand into the earth beside them to illuminate their conversation. The night was warm and overhead nightjars flitted through the branches.

'You're not used to company, are you?' Curillian had studied the young armist's manner, full of wariness and unease, and wondered how aware the stranger was of it himself.

'I am not often in company, Your Majesty…' Curillian waved a hand.

'No, no need for titles…'

'…and certainly not company of this sort.' Curillian knew the guards of the cohort had given him a hard time, but he said nothing.

'And you don't ride, do you?' The other shook his head. The king fell silent then, leaving his companion unsure where the questions were leading.

'Of course,' the king said abruptly, 'none of my armists think you should be here.' His companion tensed, thinking he was about to be turned adrift. 'They don't understand why you've been brought,' the king continued, 'and I would tell them, except I don't understand myself.' He paused. 'But since you are here, you may as well tell me your name.'

'Roujeark.'

'Roujeark,' the king repeated thoughtfully. 'What does it mean?'

'I don't know for sure. Someone once told me it meant 'Red Journey'. It is apt enough.'

'Red Journey,' repeated the king. 'That would be *Rutharth*.' Roujeark started at that pronunciation, which he had only heard once before. The king seemed not to notice. 'You must come from the mountains to pronounce it *Roujeark*. From near Arton?'

'The Upper Tribune Valley.'

'Ah,' smiled the king. 'Not too far off, then. Red I see you have in abundance from your garments…'

'Red was the only dye we had…'

'But why 'Journey'? Why did your father and mother name you so?' Curillian's perceptive eyes saw the sadness creep into the younger armist's face. It was even a sadness he could pinpoint – he had been there himself.

'I barely remember my mother. My first journey was forced upon me the night my father died.'

Again, the burning cottage and the desperate flight into the night blazed into his mind. Stronger than it had been for many years, the memories surged up. The last moments they had had together were spent frantically packing the pony's saddlebags. Roujeark had heard about the unfortunate death of the two children, swept away by the provoked river, a spell gone horribly wrong, but he had never thought it would come to this. The villagers wanted revenge, and his father had seemed resigned to it. But he had been determined that his son would escape and live his life. So he had spent the last minutes of his life in a frantic rush. Roujeark had seen the long line of torches advancing up the hillside to their home, peeking through the window, and he had got out only just in time. Tekka, their only pony, had barely carried him out of the yard when he wriggled off his back and looked back. Hiding behind an arm of rock, he could just see back down the winding path to the rear of his home.

The sounds were still alive in his mind. Angry shouts twisting in the wind…glass breaking…door crashing open…the grunts and shouts of a struggle. No anguished death-cry; only the heavy slump of a body to the floor. Then the rush of flames as the torches took hold in the furnishings, and the smashes as bottles and jars were thrown from the shelves.

The sounds were not just still alive: they throbbed in accompaniment to the inseparable images. Partners in his recurrent nightmare, together they were engraved in his heart. The dark interior of the mountain-cottage suddenly lit up with an orange glare… the shadows of many figures moving around inside…the confused shades of the struggle…the uprush of the flames, filling his wide-eyed gaze. Shock, and terror, but he hadn't been able to move. It had only been when the attackers had come to the back door, coming for him, that he remounted the pony and took flight. That black night, with all its chill wind, hadn't been able to cool the burning pain he took with him.

Feeling the hot tears streaming over his cheeks, he cuffed at them with red sleeves.

'Perhaps he foresaw it,' said he, almost to himself.

'Your pain is still near,' said the king, 'like a branding just administered. You have carried it with you all these years, with no one to tell, and it has multiplied in the carrying. Share your story with me – perhaps it will help? What happened that night?' Roujeark didn't know where to begin, and thought he couldn't bring himself to speak of it – it had been bottled up for so long – but after the first few tentative words it bubbled out like an unblocked spring.

'My father was Dubarnik...He was known in the valley as a magician...someone with power over the unseen. They supported him...us...because he was of use to them, and life seemed good. But then two children died when he made the river rise up. He was only trying to test a new device for harnessing the water's power, but it got out of control. He never told me the details, but I never thought he'd done anything wrong. Yet he blamed himself. He changed, and in the last few days he was silent and withdrawn, guilt-struck. The villagers blamed him too, and one night they came. They came with torches, fresh from the alehouse and eager for a blood-debt to be settled. My father became energised again only just in time to get me out of there, but no sooner had I left than they broke in. I never saw him fall, but I think I heard it. Then they set fire to our home, and ever since my father's ashes have lain among the ashes of our home. I have not been back.' Tears streamed out while he spoke, but so compassionate was the king's face that he did not feel abashed to weep before a stranger. By the time he had finished speaking they had dried up, leaving wet stains on his cheeks.

'And what was the journey?' the king asked.

'To Oron Amular.' The charged words lingered in the air and hung between them in the firelight, like sparks that would not go out. The king continued his questions.

'Why would an orphaned child from the Carthaki foothills seek out the Mountain of High Magic?' Across forty years, Roujeark heard his father's words again.

'You have a gift, young one, a special strain of the powers that run in our family. I may not be the mighty wizard I once hoped to be, but you have far more potential than I ever had. I have enough skill to recognise that, and I believe that, with the right tutelage, you could become great. You have great things in your future.'

'My father had some magic, and he saw it in me too. Although magic led to his death, he still hoped I could find training and become a real wizard.'

'And you came there? How did you know the way? No one knows the way, not even I, veteran of many adventures. Not many even among the elves know now, and they tell no one.'

'Prélan guided me. He led me by secret ways from the Aravell River.' Mistaking the king's pensive gaze for disbelief, he pressed his case. 'If you do not believe me, then why did you bring me this far?'

'I do believe you, Roujeark. I know what it is to be led by Prélan, and I have some skill in perceiving His hand on others. If nothing else, I can discern honesty in an armist, and I see it in you. But the real reason I brought you, if you want to know, is because I was told to. I was told to protect someone, '*for he is needed at the Mountain.*' I believe that someone is you.'

'Prélan spoke to you?' The relief on Roujeark's face was like rain on parched ground.

'Yes. Tell me how he spoke to you.'

Roujeark thought back into the happenings of that long-ago journey. 'I had just reached the land of Kalimar,' he began slowly. 'I hadn't been long in that land before an elf found me and warned me that I shouldn't be there, that it would go badly with me if I didn't leave. He frightened me. I somehow found the courage to go on, but not long after I was drawn into the woods away from the road. In a small dell I came across an old elf, or at least what I thought was an old elf...'

Looking down into the dell, seeing all the broad, short trees, bushes and patches of fern, Roujeark felt that he had found a sanctuary for the night, but then he noticed the figure sitting hunched at the foot of a tree on the dell's far side, facing him. He gave a start, and would have turned back immediately towards the road, but the person smiled. He was like, and yet unlike, the elf who had accosted him. He was dressed in a cloak and hood of peculiar colour, a deep shade that seemed to shift between green and brown, and he clutched a staff in his hands between his drawn-up knees. His smile was warm.

'Don't mind me,' said he. 'This is my dell, but I'm happy to share it with you tonight.' Drawn by the warmth in the stranger's voice, Roujeark led Tekka cautiously down to the dell's bottom until they were only a few paces from the seated figure. Roujeark could not decide whether the person was elf or armist or something else entirely. He seemed old, but had an ageless handsomeness in his face and eyes as deep as the sea.

'I'm afraid,' he began timidly, surprising even himself that he was confiding in this stranger unbidden. 'I think that...that there are...'

'That there are elves after you?' the person finished for him, and smiled. 'Yes, I know, but do not fear, they will not find you while I am here.' Roujeark's knees buckled with relief, but a thread of worry tugged at him.

'Are you staying?' The person smiled again, apparently with a power to flood him with peace.

'I don't usually,' he said, 'but tonight my special vigil shall be here. Quiet now, unpack your things and settle down. You may sleep for the time being and have no fear.'

Roujeark did so, and slept for many hours with more rest than he had ever before experienced, but sometime in the middle of the night he awoke to the sound of hooves and the soft jingling of harness. He looked up over his blanket at the dell's lip and saw three riders standing there. He began to panic, but when he looked up at the cloaked figure still sitting beside him, he saw that his face was completely unconcerned, almost as if he was not aware of the horses. Roujeark felt calmer, but was still afraid, for the riders seemed to be looking straight at him. His fears vanished, though, when they turned and rode away, leaving him unmolested. He looked up again at his guardian, who was still serenely unperturbed.

'Please,' he began, 'how did those riders not see me?' His companion gazed in front of him, not looking down.

'The elves know this land almost as well as the land knows itself, and very little that goes on in it escapes their notice, but I am able to make things blind to them when there is need.' Roujeark thought for a moment.

'What need is there?' he asked. His companion seemed not to hear the question, but instead remarked,

'It is as well that you are awake, for now you must leave this place.' Roujeark's face fell.

'So soon? Why?'

'There are things you need to see, someone you need to meet.' Obediently, Roujeark rolled up his blankets and packed them away again in Tekka's saddlebag. The old stranger got up and made to leave, but Roujeark pressed him with one last question.

'Please, I must know. Why did you help me tonight?' The hooded figure turned and looked at him. His words were as incisive and knowing as his eyes.

'You are going somewhere, and it is important that you get there. Therefore, it would have been a pity if the elves had been able to carry you back to your own country. No, they must share their land with you for a while. But come, the night passes, and there is much left to do. That way lies your path.' Following his point, Roujeark saw moonlight illuminating a path through the trees as they climbed the slope outside of the dell. When he looked back, his helper was gone. He followed the moonlit path further up the hillside. He had not gone far when he came to a little tree-shaded hollow. A little stream was issuing from a rocky surface and falling into a pool. And on the surface of the pool was a single flame, broad and incandescent. He marvelled, for no steam rose from the water, and no oil or fuel lay on the surface to feed the flame. The heat issuing from it, however, was unmistakeable. His curiosity overcame his incredulity and he took faltering steps towards it. He came to the pool's edge and reached out to touch the water, but a voice checked him. It was as terrifying and benign as the flames whence it came.

'Roujeark! Roujeark!'

'I am here,' he heard himself say, though he had barely been aware of the urge to speak.

'Do not touch the water, for this is a holy place.' Roujeark shrank back, but hearing the compassion in the deep voice, which stirred a recent memory into faint familiarity, he dared to speak.

'Please, Lord, who is it that speaks from the fire and the water? And how do you know my name?'

'I am Prélan, the God of your fathers, who was at the Beginning and who brought all things into being. I know the name your father gave to you, and I know the name I myself have for you. I know the cares of your heart, and its ambitions. You are seeking Oron Amular, but you do not know the way. Be reassured, child, for none ever come to this place and leave it still astray. Verily you are destined to go to the Mountain of High Magic, and I have drawn you here so that I might confirm you on your course and guide you.'

'I am glad, Lord, to meet you, and to receive your reassurance. I was glad also of he who watched over me this night when the elves came looking for me. But I am alone in a strange land, far from home, and without help or companions, and I am afraid.' The flame waxed larger and absorbed his vision.

'Look at this flame and know me, Roujeark. Now that we are met, you shall not lack for help or companionship again. I shall send more besides in the time to come. First, know me. Second, know that I created you and knew you before your conception; know that I love you and that I have plans for you. Plans to prosper you and to use you, for you shall grow strong. You shall confound the counsels of the wise and shake the towers of the mighty. Go forth knowing these things and take them in earnest of other things which shall be taught to you. Go back to the road with the first light of day, and there you shall meet a merchant's family. They are expecting you, and they will carry you as far as the Aravell Bridge. There we will meet again.'

'That was my first encounter with Prélan,' Roujeark concluded. Curillian sat entranced by the retelling.

'Your first?' the king asked, rousing himself from his absorption. 'What were the others?'

'I found the merchant's family, and they took me to the Aravell Bridge. There I was at a loss for what to do next, but when I took refuge under the bridge, hiding from more elves, I met Prélan again…'

The water's reflection flickered on the underside of the bridge. At first it was dim, but then the patterns grew in brightness and colour, though Roujeark could not tell where the light came from. As he watched, mesmerised, the patterns began to coalesce and produce a concerted shape. He was fascinated to see that it took on the vague but unmistakeable outline of a head. It was neither wholly elven nor armist in appearance, but it was seemingly generated by a power within the water. Then He spoke.

'Roujeark, welcome. Well done for trusting me, for you have come here, just as I asked.' Roujeark could think of no response, but had to cower slightly and cover his eyes, for the shape seemed to gather brightness as it spoke. The voice was soft, but in the confines under the bridge it seemed to boom and echo. 'Do not worry,' said Prélan, assuaging his unspoken fear, 'the elves will not overhear us. Indeed, they will again be blind to you as soon as you leave the cover of this bridge, where their eyes are most watchful.' Roujeark plucked up his courage and spoke, though still unable to look directly at the lights.

'Lord, is it still to Oron Amular that I go?'

'The Mountain waits for its last son. This is where you leave the road, and follow the Maker's paths on the last leg of your journey. The directions are written in the water: drink, and know.' Roujeark looked down, and was amazed to see foreign characters lingering amid the river's rippling current. Falling to his knees, he cupped his hands and drank deep. Instant revitalisation flushed down him, and a new confidence. 'See?' said the voice above him. 'My ways are now your ways. Follow them, and reach your destination. And remember, I will always be with you…' Straightaway, the symbols in the stream vanished and the lights dimmed. They seemed to drain into the current and rush away, like a spirit of the waters. Yet he could still feel the glow of some of it within his belly.

A look of rapture was on the king's face. A slight note of envy was in his voice when he spoke again.

'You are lucky to have heard Prélan speak in such a manner twice. I myself have only heard His voice audibly on one occasion, and I thought I was blessed indeed to have had just that. Yet ever after, throughout my life, I have heard His voice in other ways, and felt my feet guided by His paths. So you came to the Mountain?'

'Yes,' said Roujeark, 'but first I had a strange encounter…but it is late…'

'The moon has barely risen,' said the king. 'I will not be able to sleep until you have told me the end of your tale.'

'Very well. Climbing into the mountains, guided I know not how by Prélan, I came to a mysterious cave…'

Compelled from within, Roujeark entered into the cave, tugging a reluctant Tekka along with him. The cave inside was like a tunnel, comfortably high enough for him to walk un-stooped, and sufficiently broad for him and Tekka to walk abreast. After some time, the passage forked and went into two separate tunnels. At the end of both tunnels, there was a door, of standard size and shape, not unlike that of his old home. The final direction came from within him, like a voice issuing up his throat.

'There are two ways, and you must choose between them. One way will lead you to the answer, and the other will not. Trust not to your eyes, but rather listen to your heart, and follow it, even if the way seems uncomely.' He pondered the words and looked from one door to the other. As he got nearer, he saw that the door on the left was very well-made from varnished pine. It was bound with gold and a warm reddish glow issued from the cracks around it. The passage leading up to it was warmer and seemed much more inviting. The door on the right, however, was not so stately. The scarred and singed wood was falling apart and great holes were torn into it. It was hung with icicles, jagged and menacing, and the whole tunnel leading up to it was frosty and repellent.

He stood looking at the doors, turning from one to the other. The door on the left seemed so nice and warm and looked so comfortable. The heat issuing from it seemed to draw him closer so that he was several steps down the tunnel before he realised it. As he went, he expected the heat to increase, but instead the air about him grew colder. Soon he was shivering, and his breath was misting in front of him. His confidence peeled back like a curtain, and panic rose within him. His flesh broke out in goose-pimples and he shook violently, but still the door ahead looked so appealing that he strove to get to it. After another few painful steps, however, he began to notice that the door was not as well-made as it had first appeared. A veneer of finesse seemed to strip away, leaving a rotten, dejected layer underneath. He stepped quickly away, disappointed, and retraced his painful way back to the fork in the tunnel. Panting, and doubled up, he despaired to look at the two doors again: one harsh and cold, and the other whose magnetism he now knew was deceptive. He remembered what the voice had told him: trust not to your eyes, but rather to your heart. He breathed deep and decided to try the right-hand passage.

He steeled himself for another ordeal, and indeed, the first few steps in the right-hand passage was like trying to walk through a blizzard. Deadly cold clutched at him, but his heart was calm, completely against his better judgement. A few more steps and suddenly the fierce edge of the cold abated and the going became easier. Daring to look up, he noticed a change in this door also. The holes filled up, the singes disappeared and the wears of use and signs of neglect slowly faded. He traced his fingers against the passage wall, and what had at first been icy-burning to touch now became warm. The temperature in the passage was increasing rapidly, until, a few steps from the door, the walls were too hot to touch. Yet this time, instead of feeling more panicky as the temperature changed, he felt a warm sensation of peace spreading through him. His face flushed, and by the time he reached the door, he felt the homely heat that one might experience in the bath. On closer inspection, the door before him was the picture of finery, as if before he had viewed it through a distorting cobweb of filth, hiding the magnificence beneath. Hesitantly, he reached out and touched the doorknob. It stung his hand like a glowing coal. Yet as he held it, restraining his initial impulse to let go, he felt the heat reduce to a comfortable, reassuring heat. His other senses suddenly reported contentment too: his nose smelt fragrant, newly-cut wood, and his ears heard pleasant, yet indistinct sounds. Twisting the knob, he pushed the door ajar and went through.

Half expecting to be greeted by some impenetrable darkness, he found himself dazzled instead by some great light in front of him. As he stepped through fully and shut the door behind him, the light gradually subsided and he saw that he was in what looked like a garden. It was filled with the fragrance of flowers and trees and plants grew everywhere. The place was alive with colour so vivid that it hurt his eyes at first: orange, blue, yellow, red, green and turquoise. He heard the trickle of water and saw that a small but crystal clear stream was flowing over a succession of waterfalls. A very tall figure, all in white with hands clasped behind him, had his back to him. His garments were of the purest white, trimmed with gold, and upon his brown hair was a plain circlet of gold. When he turned, Roujeark beheld a face of astonishing handsomeness. It was dominated by golden-brown eyes which radiated warmth and power. As he approached, Roujeark found himself barely level with the other's waist, and forced to crane his neck to look up at him.

'Who are you?' was all he could ask, in a tone of wonder.

'I am a messenger from Prélan Arrion, The Lord Almighty. You may call me Ardir.' His voice was like rhythms of deep music, soft and noble. 'You have chosen well, son of Dubarnik, and to have come this far has proven your wisdom and worth.' Roujeark felt abashed, unsure what to say next.

'Truly, I am glad to be here, though I did not expect to find such loveliness at the end of such an unpromising route.'

Ardir smiled. 'Verily. Oft the more attractive way proves hardest, while the harder-seeming leads to unexpected rewards.'

'I don't know if it was all some kind of test for me, but it seemed that I had to shun the obvious path, and take the one which looked harder. I feel sure that only such wisdom as Prélan has given me enabled me to choose aright. By myself, I'm sure I would have gone astray. Ever since I first met Him at the pool He has been with me.' Ardir smiled at his words, the smile of one whose hopes have been fulfilled.

'You do well to pay homage to your Maker. Assuredly, I have watched Him guide you, and bestow upon you the right measures of humility and courage. Having passed through then, come, and see what I was bidden to show you.' He led Roujeark around the garden to a place where suddenly the ground came to an end. They were on a cliff, with clouds just above them. Looking down, they could see the land of Kalimar far below, spread out like a living map.

Roujeark had seen impressive vistas from mountaintops before, but this surpassed them all; he could even see parts of Maristonia, whence he had come. However, it was the Black Mountains which dominated his view, a dense thicket of jagged slopes and white-tipped peaks. He saw armies of trees on their slopes that eventually marched down into the great Ankil woods. He saw the other forests of Kalimar, mighty and humble alike, and glinting silver waterways threading their way through field and valley. Most captivating of all, he saw the sea for the very first time, where sunlight danced on its waves. Following them to the shore, he saw a great river plunge into a bay of golden sands and pure white cliffs. It truly was a beautiful land.

'Behold Kalimar,' declared Ardir, 'most beautiful of all lands. I rejoice in its beauty while I may, for soon I shall grieve for her.'

'Why do you say that?' inquired the armist, suddenly filled with curiosity and a foreboding of great sadness.

'Because, alas, the foremost fingertips of a great shadow are already groping at its edges; a great storm is brewing away north. If the storm itself can be withstood, the floods which come after may prove irresistible.' Up until then he had been gazing, like Roujeark, out at the magnificent landscape, but now he turned to look at him, and his face was very grave.

'This is the story which you are caught up in, and, as the Lord Prélan has decreed, your part will soon be made clear to you.' He took from his robes a piece of folded parchment and clasped it against the armist's smaller hand. 'Now it is right for me to give you this, to light the next steps.'

Opening it up, Roujeark eagerly anticipated a replica of the panorama beneath his feet, but no, it was...blank. He opened his mouth to speak, but Ardir spoke first. 'It is not as other maps, made to quench the beholder's curiosity all at once; yet nevertheless, it will guide you true, step by step.' Again, Roujeark made to speak, but Ardir held up a forestalling hand. 'More than that I cannot say. Trust in Prélan and he will not lead you astray.' And with that, he seemed to fade before him. Even as he looked, Ardir dematerialised and vanished into thin air. Roujeark blinked, and the world about him reverted to what it had been.

'You have spoken with Ardir?' Curillian was amazed, and Roujeark was not able to appreciate how difficult it was to amaze an armist like Curillian. 'Depending on your theological bent, some would account that a third meeting with Prélan...and...in person. Though whether he be Prélan incarnate, or one of His angels, I do not know. Your life has indeed been marked out in a special way, Roujeark, son of Dubarnik. But come, finish your tale. Ardir's map guided you to the Mountain...?'

'It did. I set out hesitantly from there, all too aware that the map in my possession was blank. Walking in one direction, I found that the map remained blank, and so too for another direction, but when I tried a third, walking towards the setting sun, I saw that the map came alive. A dusting of colour blushed a tiny portion of it, showing the slopes across which I walked. The remainder of the crumpled page stayed resolutely blank, and if I wavered to one side or the other, it ceased to expand, but as long as I proceeded in the correct direction, it followed my feet.

'One day I was shown just how perfectly my path had been picked out for me. I finally breasted a long, steep escarpment, and what I saw from there took my breath away. Spread out before me were the Black Mountains, in all their formidable ranks. They are aptly named, composed of the darkest stone, like a sheet of obsidian crumpled and riven into a thousand peaks, folds and crevices. Almost the only colours among them were the crowns of snow mantling the tallest peaks, and the glint of sapphire waters in hidden recesses among their feet. They extended almost as far as I could see, but due south of me I could glimpse where steep valleys tugged them down into the plains of Kalimar. Surely, I thought, if I had come any other way, I would have had to find a path through that granite wilderness. Had Prélan brought me so far east with the merchant's family to circumvent those difficult passes, setting my feet on easier tracks instead?

'The sun, having cast a reddish tint over the dark mountains, had set behind a particularly high massif, but then, almost in a display for me, it peeked savagely out. The parting shot scorched the knotted landscape, but in one place, at the corner of my vision, it set it spectacularly ablaze. I turned to look, and gasped in awe. Was that a mountain with its entire top-half aflame? The vast ice-sheets and snowfields on one enormous mountain were rippling and shimmering with flames, captivating me. The great mountain stood apart from the rest, rearing like the neck of a proud horse far above the thin spur which connected it to the rest. Not only did it stand apart in location, but it soared twice as tall as any others which were in view. It dominated the skyline so effortlessly that I was amazed I had not seen it before. It reached up so high above the ridge in front of it that it looked like a vast tower enclosed by a garden fence. I blessed Prélan in my heart for arranging this perfectly clear evening in which the mountain could be seen in all its glory. My mind slowly caught up with my eyes. Could it be? Intuition built upon suspicion until my disbelief came crumbling down, and my knees with it. Oron Amular. This was what I had journeyed so far to see. Then the flames on the mountain's sides began to die down. Suddenly, the sun vanished and the great mountain was dowsed in darkness.

'So it was that I came to Oron Amular, and the sight of it alone made the whole journey worthwhile. Getting down to the mountain, however, was no easy task. The mountain seemed to grow no nearer, no matter how many ridges I scaled, or how many dales I traversed. Tugging Tekka along with me made the task much harder. I spent several days trying to get closer to it, and seemed to make only slight progress. Each evening I hoped for another sunset to kindle the snowy peak and recreate the vision of that first sighting, but each evening my hopes were denied by overcast skies. However, despite the cloud cover, the early summer air was hot and humid. Pausing at a shoulder of rock which offered a tantalising view of my destination, I wiped my brow clear of sweat and wondered how much further to go that night.

"Will I ever get there?" I said aloud to myself.

"Where is it you are going?"

"The Mountain, of course." I made the reply before realising that it was not I who had asked the question. I had been on the road for two months now, with only minimal contact with people, so I assumed that any voice I heard was either my own, or Prélan's within my head. Now, with a shock, I realised otherwise, and whirled around. It took a moment for me to spot him, but then I saw him, an old man sitting on a flat-topped rock, staff between his knees. The old man's dark purple robes blended in with the rock behind him, but his pale face and long wispy white hair stood out.

"Who, who are you? And what are you doing here?" I asked nervously. The old man seemed bemused.

"I live here. I am out for an evening stroll." He pointed a bony finger at me. "No, more to the point is, what you are doing here." He drew his hand back into the folds of his robes and settled himself for an answer. He seemed relaxed, but his eyes watched me ever so carefully. I shivered under the intense scrutiny, but I swallowed hard and decided to start from the beginning.

"I was sent here." The old man waited patiently for more elaboration. "Some time ago," I went on, "I lost both my father and my home on the same night." Was that the barest softening of the eyes, betraying some compassion? "Before he died, my father told me to seek out Oron Amular." I shrugged. "I know nothing of the place but the name." The old man leaned forward interestedly.

"Who was your father, I wonder, to have directed you thus?" Tears formed in my eyes as I brought my father to mind.

"He was a magician," was all I could say.

"A magician," the old man repeated thoughtfully. "Hmm, did he tell you anything about Oron Amular?"

"I had but the vaguest directions, knowing only that it lay in Kalimar, somewhere beyond the Delarom Pass, and I believe I am near its slopes now. Many weeks on the road, across fields and over hills, have brought me to this place."

"So, you come from beyond Delarom Pass? Then you are, as you appear to be, a son of Armanor?"

"I am an armist, yes."

"Maristonia is a long way from here. With such vague directions, how did you come to make it this far?"

"I had help," I said simply. "An elven family bore me through Kalimar in their wagon, and…" I paused, suddenly embarrassed by what I was about to say.

"And…?" the old man prompted me.

"And I think Prélan appeared to me several times, guiding me." The old man's eyes lit up, along with his whole face.

"Ahhh," he exhaled expressively. "One who comes in the name of Prélan is to be welcomed." He resumed his scrutiny of me, and after a few moments' thought, he pronounced, "I think your father sent you here because he wanted you trained; because he believed you had some talent with magic." I nodded, for that made sense.

"Whenever he worked magic and performed tricks, he always used to say I had greater powers than him. I didn't believe him."

"Did you not?" the old man mused. "And you do not know elvish? Not even enough to know that in elvish, Oron Amular means 'Mountain of High Magic'? No? Well, the training would be long indeed." He broke off, muttering to himself. "Many have heard of my Mountain…"

"It's your mountain?" I interrupted excitedly.

"Yes, it is *my* Mountain. Many have heard, but your father would appear to be among the few who guess that a fraternity of magic still lingers on here." Then he dropped his voice so low that I could barely hear him. "Perhaps it is you then…" He looked up and raised his voice to a more audible level again. He seemed to be in the grip of some strange emotion and had to clear his throat to regain his composure. "Tell me, what is your name?"

"Roujeark, sir. If it is your mountain, can you take me there?"

"And tell me, Roujeark," asked the old man, ignoring my question completely, "what does your name mean?"

"In the language of my land it means 'red journey', though I have never understood why." The old man chuckled, a sound strangely at odds with the sad kindness in his face.

"That is but an armist corruption of *Rutharth*, the Journey of Red. You are garbed in red, and your hair is red, but this is your first real journey. There are many reasons why the journeys ahead of you will be red, but that is not for you to know now." His voice deepened and his gaze took on a faraway look as he made this pronouncement. Then he seemed to remember my question. "And yes, I could take you to my Mountain, but it would do you little good, I am afraid. Soon it will be empty, and to go whither its inhabitants are bound would be far too perilous for an untrained youth such as yourself. Alas, weightier concerns have conspired to make this first journey of yours futile. But," he said, surveying his visitor with that unsettling intensity again, "it may be that there are things for you to do first, just as I myself have a grave task at hand. No, now is not your time."

My heart sank. The muggy evening turned suddenly chill, and a sudden weariness swamped me.

"But I've come so far, wasted so much time…" The old man raised his eyebrows.

"Is time something you are short of? Do others demand of you?"

"I have nowhere else to go," my voice was pleading now. The old man smiled sadly, but he was resolute.

"No, I can understand that this is a bitter blow for you, but now is not your time." Something in the old man's face cleared, as if a knotted problem had suddenly resolved itself. 'You will come here again," he declared with confidence, "but I see now that it will be in company. Very esteemed company, I think." He rose creakily to his feet, hauling himself upright with his staff. A strange red flash lit the sky by the mountain, and he looked impatiently towards the mountain, and then down again at me. His face softened, and he laid a tender hand on my red hair.

"Be blessed, *Rutharth.* You have done well to follow Prélan's promptings so far, see to it that you continue to do so. He has a place and a plan for you. And wait for my sign – then you will know that your time has come." He muttered some strange words over me, though whether it was a prayer or a benediction of some kind, I don't know. Then he pushed something into my hand. "When you come back, bring this with you as a token to any that might challenge you. Until then, son of Dubarnik, be blessed..." The hand lingered a moment, quivering as it imparted something that made my hair tingle, and then it was withdrawn. I closed my eyes in despair, and let tears course down my cheeks. When I opened them again, the old man was gone, with only the receding sounds of his footsteps remaining. The deepening night around me seemed to reflect my mood, but then suddenly I started, realising that I had not told the old man my father's name – how had he know it was Dubarnik? As I thought this, a surge of power, like a jolt of excitement, electrified every part of me.

'I slept that night at the place of my meeting with the old man, whose name I had not even learned. I felt very small in that landscape of giants, and very alone. I thought to delay my return journey at least until the light came, yet it was not the light of day which woke me, but a flickering of strange colours. Rising, I went to the overlook again, and in the darkness, I saw flashes of blue, green and red which illuminated the sides of the mountain. They were like the flash I had seen during my conversation with the old man the evening before. Eerie and comforting at the same time, they illuminated a small column issuing forth from some hidden door in the mountain. More flashes seemed to emanate from the column itself. As that column made its way north, like an army on its way to war, I prepared to make my own journey.'

Roujeark completed his tale at long last and looked up at Curillian, whose attention had never wavered.

'That is how I came to Oron Amular. I still do not know who that old man was, but I still have what he gave me…' He drew forth from his pocket a metal star, engraved with runes and decorations in intricate detail. Curillian gasped when he saw it.

'A Seal of the League of Wizardry. Do you realise this is probably the first time one of these has been seen outside of the Mountain since the Second War of Kurundar? Phew, even if I had doubted your tale up until now, this would confirm everything. The wizards each used to carry one of these, a token of authority and membership of the League of Wizardry, but now they must be among the rarest and most valuable trinkets in the world. Incredible! Why did you not show it to me before, when we first met in Mariston?'

'I had forgotten all about it,' said Roujeark truthfully. 'Telling my story for the first time reminded me.' Curillian ran his hands over the star.

'The old man you met was Kulothiel himself, I feel sure.'

'Kulothiel?'

'The Head of the League of Wizardry, and Keeper of the Mountain. He is a great power. An ancient man now, but he has long been the mightiest mage in Astrom. Yet the world has forgotten him, for he seemed to have forgotten the world. Verily, Roujeark, you are vindicated in seeking me out. I am indeed on my way to Oron Amular, summoned to a tournament there. But until I met you I had no clear idea, other than a couple of unpromising leads, about how to get there. Could you lead me there, by way of the Aravell?' Roujeark just nodded dumbly, slightly bewildered by the pace of the conversation and the strength of the king's sudden resolve. 'The elves won't like it, of course,' Curillian went on, 'but that's a problem for another day. So you will guide me, and I will protect you. Thus shall we serve each other, just as Prélan clearly intended.'

The king went quiet again, lost in thought. At first Roujeark thought the conversation was over, but something made him stay. Intrigue about this strange king, so gentle yet so formidable, so rough yet so deep, so simple yet so mysterious, was growing in him. Curillian, who had done most of the scrutinising so far, was surprised to find himself on the receiving end.

'What?' he asked gently. Roujeark seemed bashful.

'Oh, nothing. Well, it's just...you're not quite as I imagined the king would be.' Curillian smiled, having heard similar assessments many times.

'Really? And what do you imagine the king should be like?'

'I don't really know,' confessed Roujeark, embarrassed. 'But in the hills where I grew up, we have heard two things about the king. One says that his strength is legendary, that he is tall as an elf and brave as a hero. The legends of his deeds all speak of great feats and daring exploits.' Curillian smiled at this description of himself. He was at least six inches too short to be even a short elf. 'The other thing we have heard is that he is very aloof, very remote, too grand to be approached.' Again, Curillian smiled.

'That last part sounds more like my father Mirkan than myself. So you think I am not like these stories you have heard?'

'You are obviously a great warrior,' Roujeark said, struggling to find the right words, 'but your strength seems more down to earth than legend makes it. I mean, how many kings would take the time to sit down like this and talk to a simple peasant? You are more… well, accessible.'

'How many simple peasants would talk thus to a king?' rejoined Curillian. 'It seems we are neither of us as we ought to be.' The king lapsed into a long, deep silence. The brand crackled softly and in its light, Roujeark saw the far-away look in the king's eyes. It came as a surprise to him when, after a long time, the king spoke again. He was even more surprised when he heard the words which were spoken.

'I too was forced to make a long, hazardous journey when I was only young, and I too lost my father before I really knew him. An evil counsellor of my father, the erstwhile Lord Protector, caused me to be sent into exile and usurped the throne that should have been mine. Unlike many princes who have come to kingship through ease and privilege, I only attained it after long years of labour and testing. I wandered through Dorzand and Ciricen and Aranar, never knowing a true home. I was an outlaw, fending for myself and encountering many strange people and places. Later I came to Ithrill and there entered the service of the Silver Emperor, Lancearon. He gave me the name Ruthion.'

'Why Ruthion?' Roujeark interrupted without meaning to. Curillian seemed unperturbed – indeed, he even seemed to think the question significant.

'It means 'Red Warrior'. I wore red armour and apparently reminded the elves of one of their heroes from older days. Anyway, as Ruthion I kept safe the borders of the Silver Empire, fighting many enemies. When the Second War of Kurundar broke out, I fought in that conflict too, first in the emperor's cavalry, and later with my own army. After I recovered from a deadly wound, the time was deemed ripe for me to reclaim the throne of Maristonia, whose strength the empire so badly needed in that desperate war. I returned to Maristonia, and, with Prélan's help, I overthrew the tyrant Lord Protector and won back my throne. After leading the Maristonian Army to victory in the war, I came back home to live out my days in relative peace. Here I have been ever since – more or less – and here I am, just as you find me.' He didn't know why he had told this stranger all that, but he had felt able, for some reason, to open up.

'So,' responded Roujeark tentatively, 'Red Journey and Red Warrior?'

'Yes, it sounds like we'll make fine travelling companions, doesn't it? Prélan knows what He's doing, seemingly. A lesson I find myself having to learn time and again. But I marvel at you, Roujeark, to go seeking magic, the very thing which caused your father's death.'

'At the time magic was all I had…It still is. If I can learn to use it properly, and control it, then I might be able to make up for my father's death, mightn't I?'

'Perhaps. Yet I still say you are courageous. I remember, in my very earliest days, when my brother Aramist swam for the first time – he was carried off by a swift current and nearly died. His death came not long afterwards, from a sickness, but for all his remaining days he had been terrified of water. But you, you grapple with what nearly caused your death. Whether your gift of magic proves to be a blessing or a curse remains to be seen,' said Curillian. 'The more I think about you, the more I see a heavy doom lying on your shoulders. You have become entangled with the great affairs of the world. If you are to walk the path set before you, you will need to hold tight to Prélan.' As these words sunk in, Curillian stood up, plucking the brand from the ground. 'It is late, my new friend. Get some sleep. Let us see what tomorrow may bring.'

The last thing Roujeark saw, as he walked back to the already-slumbering camp, was the old king wandering amid the trees, taking counsel with himself in the torchlight.

III
Water and Fire

THEY broke camp early the next morning. With torturously stiff legs and back, Roujeark forced himself back into his saddle. They had not gone far along the road before they stopped. Standing up in his stirrups and gazing forward, Roujeark could just see the king deliberating with the senior officers at the head of the column.

'We'll leave the road here,' Curillian told Lancoir and Surumo, 'and make for Laston.' They looked at him in surprise.

'For Laston?' asked Lancoir. 'You mean to go the long way round?'

'I do,' Curillian confirmed.

'Markest would be better,' the knight ventured tersely.

'Only if you're willing to put up with prying eyes through the whole East-fold, which I am not. No, we shall avoid the main road through the pass and go via Welton.'

'The ferry at Laston will be a far quicker way to reach Welton,' put in Surumo. 'Much easier than negotiating all the traffic on Delarom Pass.'

'Just so,' confirmed Curillian. Lancoir's misgivings showed plainly on his face.

'I hope our footpad hasn't been suggesting any wild notions or strange paths,' said he. 'The armists don't trust him. They think he is a magician of unknown powers.' Curillian gestured for Surumo to get the column moving again, and then he laid his hand on Lancoir's arm as the first riders trotted past.

'Lancoir, Prélan has spoken to me. For better or worse, we will take Roujeark to Oron Amular, and he will be our guide. Do you accept this?' Lancoir's returned his sovereign's steady gaze in silence for a while, and then nodded assent. 'Good armist,' said the king happily, slapping his captain's vambrace. 'It's just as well, really, since before meeting him our chances of finding the Mountain were slim.' Lancoir nodded in grudging acknowledgement.

'It's his idea to go via Phirmar?'

'It is no notion of his that I am following, Lancoir, but my own, so be at peace. Roujeark will guide us, but first I wish to talk to a friend in Welton. I may find out something useful. Going this way also has the added advantage of being more discreet – the whole country doesn't need to know I'm on the road. Plus, I'd rather not have news of my riding go ahead of me to reach the ears of any potential competitors. Leave them guessing for the time being. And as for the troops, they will just have to get used to Roujeark. Magician or not, he is no danger to them. Come.'

Having left the road, they made across country for a while before striking a new road. Not so large or well-maintained as the first, which was one of the main thoroughfares of the kingdom, it was nevertheless kinder to Roujeark's pain-wracked body than the rough uneven ground of the open country. This second road led them by mid-afternoon to the coast. During a noontime pause the king had sent errand riders ahead to make preparations, which meant that when the main company arrived they found the town in an uproar of excitement. A modest port of several hundred colourful stone houses, Laston's inhabitants made their living either from fishing or from trades connected to the great ferry which docked in their harbour. Many important visitors and delegations used the ferry – most notably the Duke of Welton – but the presence of the king was a rare and special occasion. Without the benefit of advance warning, the whole population had turned out of their brightly-painted houses or left their nets and lobster-cages at the waterfront and hurried to make the place ready for the royal visitor. Extra hands were assigned to make the ferry ready, and others cleared up the main street and then lined it with hurriedly cut flowers.

When the main company arrived outside the town's stockade and rode under its large, seashell-studded arch, most of the town's population was still lining the road. Making the most of this unexpected glimpse of their beloved king, they cheered him past with great enthusiasm. Similar enthusiasm was also directed at his escort, but unlike foot-slogging legionaries who might have availed themselves of the town's hospitality, these disciplined Royal Guards rode on through with professional smiles and cool reserve. Another shell-adorned arch, this time rearing out of a low stone wall, marked the entrance to the harbour area. Here the cohort dismounted and waited while the ferry was made ready. Their most strenuous task was to keep back the still-buzzing crowd who had followed them, hoping for another look at the king. Not a few of the younger guards regretted not being in their full, resplendent uniforms while talking to the town's pretty girls.

For Roujeark, it was a first close-up view of the sea. He had seen it from afar before, and smelled the salt-tanged sea breeze wafted up the River Ebinnon while in Mariston, but never had he been so close. While the cool wind was refreshing, the prospect of tossing about on waves after riding a horse filled him with consternation. Unlike the guards about him, he was not able to enjoy the beautiful setting. Large mountains loomed away to the west, representing the uttermost end of the Carthaki Mountains, whose easternmost flanks fell sheer into Dagger's Cove, the great blade-shaped inlet which separated most of Maristonia from the East-fold and Swordhilt Peninsula beyond. The sun glinted off the sea and leisurely waves broke upon the shingly beaches adjoining the harbour-wall. The guards studiously avoided contact with him, as they had on the first day's ride, despite being more curious about the stranger after his late-night conference with the king, and so, as well as dreading the voyage to come, he felt despised and lonely. If it had not been for the kindly interest the king had shown in him, together with his reassuring references to Prélan, he would be perfectly miserable by now.

Curillian, Lancoir and Surumo were met at the quayside by the Harbour-master, a tough-looking seafarer who had hastily donned a jacket in an attempt to look more respectable. He bowed clumsily to the king, and then seemed rather taken aback when the sovereign shook his hand.

'My gratitude to you for getting the ferry ready at such short notice, Harbour-master.'

''Tis no trouble, Yore Majesty. As you know we always keep one o' the ferries free for military use. I've some hands aboard now re-arranging some o' the bulkheads to make room for yore horses. If Yore Majesty will be so good as to wait a little while, we'll 'ave her ready in a brace of shakes.'

'Good,' said Lancoir. 'How many can you take in one run?' The Harbour-master thought for a moment.

'Sixty with horses, or a hundred without.' The officers discussed this.

'We won't need the horses right away on the Phirmar side,' said Surumo. 'The Tonsor barges can take us on up to the Welton Road.' Curillian nodded his assent.

'Well Commander, choose twenty lucky victims to remain behind with the horses for the second crossing. Leave your second-in-command, Piron, to command them. They will join the main body at the barracks on Welton Hill while we conclude our business in the city. See that the whole cohort is ready to ride again on the fifth morning from now, *24 Milariel*.'

'Very good, sir.' Surumo went off in search of his subordinate. Lancoir beckoned to the Harbour-master, who had been hovering nearby.

'Leave the horses till last – one hundred to go in the first crossing.'

'Aye aye,' said the Harbour-master, doffing his sun-bleached cap. Then he moved alongside the king surreptitiously. Dropping his voice, he told him, 'Are you sure you wouldn't like to wait for an escort? Well, it would seem only proper, Yore Majesty, and a-sides, there's been more than usual corsair-activity out beyond the peninsula... troubling merchantmen and the like, or so the patrols report.'

'I thank you for your concern, Harbour-master, but it will take too long to wait for a warship from Lecoin. They may be a damned nuisance, but no corsair has yet troubled the ferry, and if they do, we'll deal with any trouble.'

Curillian and Lancoir strolled onto the ferry, a great broad-bellied craft, and inspected it. It was a sparse, utilitarian vessel, its few concessions to comfort being aft cabins immediately below decks where high-ranking passengers could pass the crossing more easily. Hardly fit for a king at such short notice, but Curillian was not bothered. Above decks the ferry's masts were crammed with every yard of sail possible, for maximum speed. When the wind was contrary, as it was now, propulsion was by means of scores of oarsmen on the bottom deck. Half of them were unskilled local labourers for whom this was the best means of livelihood available; half of them were corsair prisoners put to work without pay and with considerably worse treatment. Of the three ferries in service at Laston, this was the largest, but the other two civilian craft were nowhere to be seen – presumably at sea or on the Phirmar side of the bay.

The king and his chief captain watched from the quarter-deck as the hundred chosen guards filed up the quay and across the gangplank. They quickly settled themselves on the main deck, preferring the sun-washed open air to the austere sickness-prone compartments below. Roujeark was awkwardly tagging along near the back of the line, clearly unsure as to whether he should be going as well. Piron, too, was unsure and held him back while he looked to the quarter-deck for guidance.

'What about him?' Lancoir asked of the king.

'He comes.' Lancoir waved his arm in a beckoning gesture, and Piron let the red-clad armist past.

The crossing began pleasantly enough. Although the going was slow, as the oarsmen bent their backs against the wind, the sun was out and the chance for resting was welcome. It was a fine early spring day, unseasonably warm. This was the closest a Royal Guard ever came to a holiday.

Roujeark sat apart, leaning on the ship's side and watching the waves twinkling in the sunshine. He saw patrolling fins, but was entirely ignorant of the size of the sea-creature under the surface to which they belonged.

'Sharks,' said a crewmember as he came nigh to slacken off a rope, though the name meant nothing to Roujeark. 'Our meals would be much the poorer without them.' Grinning, he left Roujeark to his solitude. He was on the starboard side, and was soon dozing in the warm sunshine. He did not know how long they had been sailing when an unusually large wave suddenly jolted him awake. Rubbing his eyes, he looked out over the azure water. His eyes reported a strange blur at the edge of sight, a sort of distortion on the eastern horizon. He blinked away the drowse, thinking he was still half-asleep. But no, there it was. Nothing distinct, just a blur like a heatwave. A stab of warning smote his heart, though he could see no reason why it had. Uneasy, he got to his feet and squinted into the distance. No one else showed any sign of concern – indeed, most were asleep on the deck – but he could not shake this sudden disquiet in his heart. Apprehensively, he approached the quarterdeck. The guard at the stairs was one of the few who were awake and alert. He barred the way resolutely.

'Please, I just need to speak to the king.'

'No one goes on the quarterdeck without invitation, least of all you.'

Curillian heard the exchange and strode to the top of the stairs. Predictably, young Roujeark was being obstructed by one of the guards.

'What's the matter, friend?' he called down. Roujeark took advantage of the guard's momentary relaxation to push past and climb a few steps.

'I…I think there's something out there,' he said, pointing out to sea. He fell silent after blurting out those words, suddenly at a loss.

Then inspiration came to him. 'A ship on the horizon.' Another ruler would have dismissed him curtly, but Curillian wasted no time in calling the captain over, who in turn bellowed up to the crow's nest. The lookout shouted down that there was nothing to be seen. Many of the dozing passengers had been roused by the raised voices, but when nothing further seemed to happen, they resumed their repose.

'Perhaps you were mistaken, Roujeark?' the king suggested. 'The sea can play tricks on inexperienced eyes.' Roujeark was thankful for the gentle way with which he was being dismissed, and knew he should step back down and leave matters be. Yet the alarm in his heart, far from dissipating with the lookout's reassurance, redoubled in conviction.

'Please, Your Majesty, I really do think there is a ship out there.' Curillian studied him carefully. Then he turned again to the ferry's captain.

'Captain?'

'If my lookout says there's nothing, then there's nothing,' the Laston armist replied stoutly. Curillian looked from one to the other. He looked at Lancoir, and to Roujeark's surprise, the captain of guards did not look sceptical, but wary. The king walked to the side and looked out himself, gripping the gunnel with powerful forearms. After painfully long seconds of deliberation, he turned around.

'Lancoir, my sword.'

'What?' the ferry-captain exclaimed, momentarily forgetting himself.

'Surumo,' Curillian issued his second command. 'Wake the cohort; make sure weapons are to hand.'

'Did Yore Majesty mishear me?'

Curillian rounded on the ferry-captain, and Roujeark saw what happened to those who abused the king's easy-going nature.

'Do you presume to question my judgement, ferry-captain?' Roujeark saw just how intimidating the king could be when roused. Taller than most armists, his powerful frame loomed over the armist from Laston, and his eyes blazed. 'If, in half an hour, my instincts are proved wrong, then you can take me to task, but until then another insolent word will have you back mending nets in Laston so fast you won't be able to swallow the salt-water on your way.'

The ferry-captain, thoroughly cowed, turned away. Lancoir re-emerged with the Sword of Maristonia, and Curillian buckled it on. On the main deck, the whole cohort had been roused and was quickly armed and ready. The decisive posture of their king up on the quarterdeck was enough to let them know danger was at hand. Yet, for a long time, nothing happened. More and more passengers began lining the starboard side, straining for some sign of life out there. The ferry-captain was looking at Roujeark as if he were crazy, but with every minute that passed, the more that expression became smugness, as of one who is about to be proved right. Roujeark was just about to slink away and try and mitigate the humiliation when the lookout's voice rang out.

'Saaaaaiiil! Saaaiil ho!' Everyone strained their eyes, but although they could not yet see what the lookout could see, the tension on deck redoubled. Roujeark just caught a glimpse of the ferry-captain looking at him before springing into action. Gone was the smugness; all there had been in that split second was sheer incomprehension. The moment passed.

'Helsman, bring her about,' the captain shouted. Curillian whirled around.

'Belay that order,' he commanded.

'Yore Majesty, there's still time to reach Laston…'

'We're not going to Laston,' the king said steadily. The crew looked nervous.

'But Yore…'

'You have your orders, captain.' Curillian rejoined Lancoir and Surumo at the gunwale. While the guardsmen streamed below decks to find weapons and armour, Roujeark went to the rail just beneath the quarterdeck, and overheard the king's conversation.

'How many on a corsair galleon?' Surumo asked.

'Two hundred at the most,' Lancoir answered tersely.

'They've got a bloody nerve,' said Surumo. 'I've never heard of corsairs molesting the ferry.'

'That's because they never have,' Curillian told him. 'They have indeed become bolder.'

'Of course, it might only be a big fisherman…Maybe we should have waited for an escort,' said Surumo doubtfully.

'No. We will get a message relayed to the fleet once we reach Welton. Right now, we have to make sure we survive and get there.'

'The corsairs will sink us from a distance with ballistas and catapults,' Lancoir said quietly to the king. 'What's your plan?'

'They won't sink us. We're no threat to them, and in their eyes we'll make a fine prize. No, they'll be greedy, and come in close. We will let them. Once they're up close, once they've grappled us, they'll find they have bitten off more than they can chew. A cohort of guards will be more than a match for a pirate mob, even if they're outnumbered. Surumo, have a dozen archers stay above decks, enough to put up a token defence – they know the ferries aren't completely helpless. Have the rest waiting below decks or hidden out of sight. Hold them back until they come alongside. Then, on my command, spring the trap.' Surumo hurried off to arrange his troops. 'I wonder how on earth Roujeark knew that galleon was out there.'

'Wizardry,' murmured Lancoir.

In no time at all the clamour had receded and all was quiet and tense on the ferry. The oars kept up their motion, but they would never outrun an enemy with the wind at his back. Their scything through the water was the only sound to be heard except the preparations of the archers. Strings were attached, bows bent, and arrows laid out. Roujeark found himself next to them, unsure what else to do. Fear was clutching his stomach and rising like bile in his throat, but he did his best to look as calm and capable as the guardsmen. Looking out he could now see plainly with his eyes the vessel which some other sense had warned him of before. Even he knew it was too big to be a fishing boat. He watched it move slowly towards them, borne nearer with every wave, and tried to quell the panic gripping him. Interminable minutes dragged by. His nerves were frayed like string across sharp rocks, and he supposed that those of the guards around him were made of steel, for they showed no sign of panic, only grim professionalism. In truth they were out of their element – they were not marines or even sailors – but they had all faced battle many times, and knew how to approach it. Roujeark, on the other hand, couldn't bear the horrible waiting when nothing seemed to be done, when he was helpless, knowing every second brought death closer, and that there was nothing he could do about it. Now he could see the emblem stamped on the other ship's sails: a white skull on a black field.

'Corsairs,' muttered the guard next to him. Roujeark turned to glance at him. He was a big armist, with a handsome face and rangy limbs that easily flexed the big bow to full draw.

'Corsairs?' The question slipped out of his lips before he remembered that he didn't want to show his ignorance.

'Aye, corsairs – you know, scum of the waves? Pirates?' Roujeark nodded, but in truth the word was a hazy one for him. As a mountain-dweller living far inland, pirates had only lurked on the edge of the wildest stories he had heard in his youth. 'They come up from Lurallan in the far south and prey on helpless tubs like us. This lot are probably from Urundair.' Roujeark blinked, surprised but pleased that one of the guards was finally speaking to him.

'How do you know all this?' he asked. The big armist smiled.

'Corsairs plagued the coast of Carinen Peninsula where I grew up, curse them! There's a couple of us in the Royal Guards who hail from the coasts.' He grinned, and then extended a big, friendly hand. 'Andil,' he said. Roujeark shook the hand uncertainly.

'Roujeark.'

'You shoot, Roujeark?' he motioned to a spare bow lying beside him.

'A bit,' he said. It was barely true, but he wanted to appear competent next to this confident warrior. He took up the bow and struggled with the string, which seemed incredibly tight to him. Andil watched him struggle for a few moments and then offered some advice.

'Kneel side on, see? Pull the string tight to your ear, and point the arrow right at your target. Breathe easy and loose when you exhale. Don't move the bow until the shaft is well away, otherwise it'll go wide.' And he demonstrated with his own bow. Roujeark flexed his bow a few times with a novice arm, but he was soon distracted by how awkward his spray-dampened robes were making the motion, and by how much closer the pirate ship had come. He thought he could even see figures hanging off the rigging, brandishing weapons and leering.

'Are we just going to wait until they're on top of us?'

'That's pretty much the thinking,' confirmed Andil. Roujeark gulped. He removed his outer robes to let him move easier, but fear made even that simple action clumsy and awkward.

'I'm sorry,' he found himself saying to Andil. 'I'm afraid I'm not much use.'

'You're doing better than the crew,' Andil reassured him. And it was true. The crew had been ordered to remain in view to make things look normal, and they shook visibly. Just then a strange snapping noise carried across the waves to them. It was followed by a long, trailing whoosh, and then, WHUMP! Something big smacked the water not far ahead of the ferry's prow. Roujeark cowered in terror. The strange succession of noises came again, and a second missile struck the water aft of the ferry, this time close enough to fling spray over them.

'What's happening?' The question came out with a shriek.

'Easy,' said Andil. 'They're firing stones from their catapult – they're only warning shots, meant to slow us down.' Orders were relayed from the king on the quarterdeck and the ferry's oars did indeed slow down. Orders also came for them to fire their bows. A pitiful volley of arrows spat across the sea between the two vessels.

'Count thirty seconds between each shot – it's only for show, see?' Andil told him. Just as well, thought Roujeark, for most of his feeble shots were just grazing the water harmlessly. All the time the pirate ship glided closer. Although she was actually the same size as the bulky ferry, her full rig of tattered sails made her seem dreadful and intimidating. Roujeark's panic kept threatening to resurface, but he fought it down each time by looking at Andil, or the king on the quarterdeck.

Now jeers and shouts could be heard across the shrinking gap. One voice, louder than the others, seemed to be ordering the ferry to stop, although Roujeark could not understand the language.

'Prepare to be boarded,' scoffed Andil, 'yeh, you can try.' Another order came and they dropped their bows and crammed against the ferry's side, hiding under the overhang of the gunwale. From there, Roujeark could glimpse the enemy ship looming up bigger and nearer through tiny holes in the wood. He could also see the king standing by the wheel. He and Lancoir stood unafraid, completely out in the open, seemingly heedless of the danger. Roujeark heard a massed creaking and many scornful voices as the pirate ship drew alongside. Slowly, Andil laid a long dagger in his hands, which Roujeark gripped like his life depended on it. He heard whirring noises, and winced as metal hooks suddenly latched onto the ferry, right above his head. His stomach lurched as the vessels came crashing together, lashed by many lines. When was the king going to do something? Was the adventure really over so soon?

One of the corsair leaders shouted down at Curillian. The king had had enough dealings with the Alanai to know their tongue, and even to discern the harsh, clipped tones of the dialect of Urundair.

'Surrender yer vessel, armist scum! Come quietly, and the Wave Brethren might be merciful.' Curillian spread his arms. The corsairs needed no further invitation, and started streaming across the makeshift gangplanks. Roujeark cowered into the overhang as many pairs of bare and booted feet crashed onto the deck in front of him. He tensed, and gripped Andil's dagger harder, knowing they would spot him any moment. The noise of whooping and screeching was horrendous. He lost sight of the king, but he heard his war-cry. Then bedlam broke loose.

'MAAAARISTONNNNN!' Had Roujeark been able to see, he would have seen how swift was the end of the first two corsairs. A group of them had approached the king, but hung back nervously. They could see his great sword and were wary of it and him. Then two of them came too close. Curillian drew the blade in the speed of a lightning-strike. Even quicker he swung it down, back up, and down again. Slash! Slash! The two corsairs fell at his feet, weapons clattering to the deck as their hands went to ripped throats. Their shipmates were appalled by the devastating speed, but before they had time to react, Lancoir struck moments after his king. Scarcely less lethal, he lunged forward and laid open the throat of another corsair. Then another terror confronted the boarders. From out of nowhere armists were appearing, streaming up on deck like swarms of ants. And not just any armists. Soldiers, warriors, armed to the teeth. The seemingly helpless ferry was now teeming with death.

Surumo had come charging up the companionway steps and burst into the open like a fiend, and at his back came roaring guard after guard. Roujeark watched as Andil and his fellow archers sprang from their hiding places and struck at the corsairs from the rear. Between them they caught their enemies in a vice of death. Deadly blows rained in from both sides. It was just as well they'd achieved surprise, though, for the guards were only able to emerge one or two at a time. Had the corsairs been expecting them, they could easily have bottled them up. As it was, the deck was soon alive with embroiled fighters. Roujeark saw the Royal Guards in action for the first time and watched the fearful efficiency with which they went about the business of killing. They employed compact, efficient motions and dealt out disciplined blows, always seeking the neck or groin. They moved with a fluidity and ease that was dreadful and hypnotic.

Roujeark was petrified at the sight of blood-thirsty corsairs, dark-skinned and brandishing cruel weapons, but his fellow passengers did not seem fazed. The noise was deafening: a cacophony of shouts, grunts, screams and curses mixed with wooden thuds, meaty smacks, sharp cracks and the ringing of steel.

The young armist's spectating was rudely interrupted when a fearsome figure appeared in front of him and blocked out the view. He had been spotted. A corsair, black-skinned but swathed in tawdry orange garments and festooned with golden jewellery, leered in at him. The snarling face ducked under the wooden overhang and beringed hands reached out for him. He cried in panic and terror, and, not knowing what else to do, thrust his dagger out and swept it back and forth with wild swings. At first he didn't realise that he had made contact, and kept on lashing out like he was battering nettles out of his path. It was only when a spurt of blood sprayed all over him that he stopped. The corsair had slumped over his legs, face and arms lacerated. He could feel the man's punctured neck leaking blood all over his trousers. The eyes rotated in unfocused rolls and the last dying breaths came in horrible, frothing gargles. Roujeark gasped and recoiled in horror.

He could now see again: the carnage on deck went on unabated. He could see Andil, swordless now, but using his arms to throw his assailants in wrestling moves. Beside him, his comrades hewed great strokes with their two-handed swords. What the guards possessed in superior skill, their foes made up for in weight of numbers and sea-canniness, and the armist defenders were hard put to it. Not so on the quarterdeck. Above the main melee, a smaller battle had been in progress. Curillian and Lancoir swept the platform like angels of death. Curillian was accomplished in combat to a degree most corsairs never imagined possible. Many of them had been drawn to the rich-looking figures by the wheel, but the king and his captain put paid to their greed and had cut them to shreds before even Surumo was able to come to their aid. When Surumo reached the king's side, with half a dozen guards, he could only gaze at the ring of bodies in awe. When he looked back over the main deck, it was now plain that the corsairs were having the worst of it. The first wave of boarders had been well-nigh slaughtered by a well-armed and well-organised trap. Victory looked assured.

One corsair had other ideas. He too watched the butchery as one after another his shipmates fell on the ferry's deck, and he could see that no effort of fighting could retrieve this disaster. His own ship would be at risk next, and he wasn't about to lose her as well as his prize. He seized a boarding pike, wrapped the haft in an oily rag and kindled it in the galley stove. With his burning spear he swung across onto the bows of the ferry where few armists were. As quick as thought, he pitched the makeshift torch down the for'ard steps and into the lower decks. No one was around to notice it, and no one was there to extinguish the flames before they got out of hand. He completed his work by stabbing an unsuspecting member of the ferry's crew in the back before hurriedly making for his own vessel again.

Andil found himself in a lull of the fighting as he suddenly looked around and found a shortage of corsairs within grappling range. The last few boarders were being hacked to the deck elsewhere, but none remained near him. Rivulets of blood stained the deck at his feet. Several of his friends lay among the pirate slain. This couldn't be it, he thought. He looked to the corsair vessel and saw many of its crew hanging back. His gaze was drawn to an agile figure dashing towards one of the gangplanks. He traced back where he had come from and saw the smoke billowing out of the companionway.

'FIRE!' he shouted. Not stopping to attend to that hazard himself, he sprinted towards the fleeing figure, looking to cut him off at an angle. With a leaping dive, he reached the corsair's running feet and pitched him to the ground. Immediately a boot crashed into his face to reward him for his trouble. In the split second's respite, the pirate made off again, swinging himself up onto the narrow bridge. Andil watched as he regained his own ship and set about hacking at the ropes lashing the vessels together. He saw the peril, and called to those around him. Curillian and others had also seen the danger and now a different kind of struggle began. The corsairs desperately tried to detach their vessel before their would-be prize became a floating inferno, and the armists shot with bows or flung daggers at the corsairs nearest them to interrupt their work.

While that struggle raged, Roujeark had been roused by Andil's initial shout. It had snapped him out of his stunned paralysis. He struggled free of the encumbering corpse and staggered unsteadily towards the nearest companionway. Stumbling down the steps, he entered the gloom below deck. It took a moment or two for his eyes to adjust to the reduced light, all the while inhaling smoke and coughing. Bodies coming the other way shoved past him and he realised that the rowers had abandoned their oars and were fleeing to the safety of the top deck. Above their clatter he dimly heard cries of panic. He grabbed one of the armists going past him.

'What's that noise – are there people still down there?'

'Only the oar-slaves.'

Roujeark looked at the armist uncomprehendingly. 'You mean you're leaving them down there to burn?'

'No better than they deserve.' The armist shook free of Roujeark's grip and carried on his way. The young armist realised he would get no help. Fighting against the torrent of fleeing rowers he ran along the deck, trying to find another companionway leading down. Already he was oppressed by the heat and choking in the smoke, and when he moved into the next compartment, he could actually see the flames. It had taken a grip in the bulkheads around it and was billowing out of control. The whole bow was ablaze and it must have already spread to the oar-deck.

At last he found the steps that would take him down. Fearing what he might find, he fearfully descended into the darkness. The heat nearly knocked him off his feet, and the overpowering stench of enclosed, exerted bodies made him gag. Through eyes made watery by the smoke, he glimpsed ahead and saw several of the for'ard-most oar-benches already wreathed in flame. He looked away in horror from the sight of blackened bodies, charred where they sat chained. He span around in a panic, not knowing what to do. As he did so pitiful cries called out to him from both sides, and he became aware of terrified oar-slaves all around him. These he could still save, but how to cut through their chains? Where were the keys? No chance to find them, so he scampered back up the steps in hunt of any implement he could use. Grabbing a hatchet from a guard's abandoned pack he swiftly returned and began hacking away at the wood around where the nearest slave's chains were secured. He made pitifully little progress, as if he were just clawing at it with his fingernails. The flames licked closer, their heat blasting him and the roiling smoke threatening to suffocate him. The wails of the oar-slaves grew ever more shrill and desperate. They would die down here, despite his efforts, and so would he if he did not leave soon. The thought that he hadn't been able to save even one pumped furious strength into his hatchet blows. Finally, moved by some deep prompting, he abandoned the hatchet and strained his hands towards the chains. He didn't even know what he was trying to do, but his fingers tingled and grew hot, and the bolts holding the chains down began to quiver. And then…nothing. They moved no further. Just then a strong hand gripped his shoulder and thrust him aside.

He looked up and through the thick smoke he recognised the stern face of Lancoir, Captain of the Guard. In the light of the flames he looked like a mercenary of hell. Lancoir swung his own axe and in a few mighty strokes had released the chains of the entire bench. As he set to another bench, Roujeark helped the released rowers clamber free of the encumbering wooden fixings, and guided them to the companionway and safety. Meanwhile Lancoir had freed another bench, and another three slaves. Roujeark knew he couldn't last much longer. Their time was up. Lancoir didn't seem to think so, for he started to hack at another bench. Roujeark tried to intervene. He threw himself on the captain, trying to restrain the blows and pull him back. He was appalled by how much stronger the knight was, and he barely interrupted his flow. He choked hoarsely. Lancoir, too, in spite of his great strength, was nearly overcome. They would have both died down there had not a squall of flames suddenly blasted them, scorching their faces and hurling them backwards. Not even hearing the final screams of the doomed slaves, together they crawled up the companionway.

Staggering along the middle deck, they remembered nothing but retching, blinding smoke and withering heat. At one point they were nearly claimed by the inferno as burning planks gave way beneath their feet, but their forward momentum just carried them past the blistering hole. Spurred to greater speed by fear of similar near-misses, they shot up the final companionway and burst back into the open air like round-shots from a cannon. Then, for Roujeark, the world screeched to a halt. His own motion was checked by some invisible force as his senses demanded his complete attention with a hasty portrait. Sunshine, heat-hazy and smoke-strewn but dazzling after the darkness. Sails flapping, smouldering. Wounded moaning. War-cries. Screams. A spear aimed and drawn back. A spear flying through the air towards Lancoir. He was allowed to glimpse this portrait for a split second before the checking force was released and the full speed of life resumed. He arched his muscles and shifted his momentum to pitch to the side. With the weight of his momentum he pushed the captain aside. The spear grazed his left arm and he crashed on top of Lancoir with a burning sensation.

The Captain of the Royal Guards stared at him, stupefied. It took him a second or two to realise what had just happened. Gratitude of feeling might have been expressed elsewise by another, but Lancoir's intensity produced a countenance akin to hatred. Roujeark thought he would strike him, but then he realised that Lancoir's blood was up and anger at his would-be killer was coursing up like magma in a volcano. Even before this thought had finished forming in the young armist's mind, he noticed Lancoir's hand reaching for the spear. In an athlete's fluid sequence of motions the captain rolled Roujeark off him, grasped the missile in a throwing grip, propelled himself to his feet, sighted the spear's former owner, span round for extra velocity and launched the projectile into the air. Mesmerised, Roujeark watched it fly through the hazy sky, even saw it wobble in its course as if unnerved by the ferocity which had flung it. A lesser being would not have been able to throw so powerfully, nor so accurately, having just come near to death in a burning chamber. But Lancoir's throw found its mark. It not only found it, piercing the pirate's incredulous heart, it carried the body right off the crossbeam it had been perching on and overboard into the sea.

The urgency of the situation allowed for no more spectating. Released from the spell of the last few seconds' events, Roujeark took in what had happened while they had been below. The corsairs, having been scoured from the ferry, had put all their effort into cutting themselves away from what would soon be a floating furnace before it engulfed their own vessel too. Curillian and his followers, though, had succeeded in keeping intact some of the bridges between the two ships. Many of the guards' cohort had already fought their way across these avenues of escape and were now fighting on the pirate galleon's decks. Lancoir was already hurrying to join them. Andil directed those of his comrades who still had arrows left for their bows to shoot down the pirates lurking in the rigging above – where they couldn't be harmed any other way – and thus shelter the other guards from the missiles being rained down. Curillian was a firestorm all in himself, the enemy resistance blown away wherever he came.

The ferry itself was barely afloat. The entire for'ard portion of it was ablaze and tilting down as fire-burned holes let the sea in. A great cloud of steam and smoke engulfed both vessels. It mattered little that the fire would soon be extinguished by a greater force, for the vessel would sink all the same. The alarming tilt of the deck brought Roujeark's predicament home to him. Rivulets of blood were running down the planks. He darted towards one of the bridges. Slower than all his travelling companions, he reached it last of all and arrived on the corsair galleon with the battle nearly over. He jumped down in comparative safety, but he now knew of a greater danger. Whilst traversing the gang-plank bridge he had seen flames from the ferry catch amid the timbers of the galleon. Despite everyone's efforts, the two ships had been together too long. Now both were doomed.

'MY KING! MY KING!' Fear made his voice carry above the vast crackling and the multitudinous din of fighting. Curillian heard it even as he clove his latest adversary almost in two. He disengaged, allowing Surumo and Lancoir either side of him to finish the job, and turned his mind to the warning cry. Straightaway he saw the threat, without Roujeark having to elaborate. He knew the vessel was doomed.

'BOATS! LONGBOATS!' he cried to those near him, gesturing at the small rowboats lashed to the galleon's decks. Furiously the ropes were cut and the cumbersome objects manhandled to the vessel's sides. The pirate crew were now too few to contest the commandeering, and even as their last members were cut down by some of their enemies, others of the guards were casting the rowboats into the sea. The armists of Maristonia worked feverishly to jettison the life-saving craft before the insatiable flames claimed them. Then, in pairs and groups, they clambered down the outside of the galleon's bulging hull and into the new craft. Beside them the sinking ferry, with her stern reared into the air and shrouded by clouds of steam, made an awesome spectacle. More and more of the guards made it overboard before the galleon too began to list. Roujeark and Lancoir were among the last to leave. With no time for the luxury of clambering, they threw themselves overboard beside one of the rowboats.

The guards in the boats were already manoeuvring with oars to pull away from the sinking ships on either side. Other oars were waved like poles to fend off burning spars fallen from the galleon. Their comrades in the water were hastily pulled into the boats, lest they be dragged down by the weight of their mail-shirts. Lancoir and Roujeark were hauled on board, the latter by the king himself. Bruised, dazed, and still struggling to breathe after their ordeal in the smoky bowels of the ferry, they lay panting in their comrades' arms. Only a few of the guards had fallen, but to an armist the survivors were battered and bloodied, sweat coursing channels through their fire-grimed faces. All they had with them were the clothes on their backs and the weapons in their hands.

'Roujeark.' The young armist was roused from his daze. Raising his head from the king's lap, he saw Lancoir sitting opposite, looking at him. It was the first word spoken between them since Lancoir had derided his offer of help in that Mariston street. Roujeark hadn't even known that Lancoir knew his name. 'You saved my life. Twice.' The words were few, but each one carried weight. Lancoir took a ring off his finger and leaned forward to press it in Roujeark's palm. It was just a simple silver band, the modest design traced on it nearly obscured by all the scratches. 'Where I come from, rings are given in token of a debt of honour. I give this to you. I will not forget until I have repaid.' Roujeark closed his hand around the ring, squeezing it, but unable to make any reply. Lancoir glanced at the king, and Curillian nodded approvingly. Then Curillian glanced in turn at each guard beside them. Humbled, they all made their gratitude known, whether it was a smile of acceptance or a comradely squeeze of the arm. Tears came to Roujeark's eyes, though whether they were from joy, relief or sheer weariness he couldn't tell. He fell back against the boat's timbers and closed his eyes as the oars pulled them out of the steam-haze and on into the long swells.

IV
The Watcher's Words

ROUJEARK awoke to find that it was nearly dark. He had dozed off in the boat and evening was in the sky. He was surprised by how cold he was. Half of the dozen guards around him were also resting or sleeping, and the other six were rowing stoically. In the front pair the king was setting a tremendous pace, rowing with great speed and endurance. Even Lancoir was struggling to match him. Truly was it spoken of Curillian that he was a great among armists, for in his veins ran the noblest blood in the land. So noble was it, some said, that it must be elvish and not armist at all. Roujeark watched him for a while, but could see no signs of him tiring. He looked about him, but the waves told him little about where they were. Behind him, the long-set sun had left a ragged red swathe across central Maristonia that was only just starting to fade. In that last ruddy light he could just make out the mountainous coast, and all that he could tell was that it seemed further away than it had before the corsair attack.

He looked at his hands and inspected them, recalling the strange impulse which had seized him below decks on the ferry. Had he been trying to work magic? Although his father had played all sorts of tricks and achieved strange effects, he himself had never even attempted magic. But the bolts had moved slightly, hadn't they? He was sure he remembered his fingers tingling, animated by a strange heat. Or was he misremembering? Had it just been the heat of the inferno? Or had his oxygen-starved brain played tricks on him? His fingers looked quite normal under his scrutiny, with nothing strange or unusual about them. He let them drop, his mind filled with new questions.

One of the resting guards manoeuvred his way forward and relieved Lancoir from his oar. As the captain came back, Roujeark ventured a question.

'How far from shore are we?' Lancoir shrugged and took a swig from one of the few canteens they had with them.

'Hard to say. The ferry can do the crossing in ten hours with the right wind, but who knows how long it takes to row?' Roujeark still felt nervous asking another question, despite Lancoir's earlier pledge.

'But do we even know where we're going?' He glanced up and saw that clouds rolling in from the ocean had covered most of the sky. There were precious few stars left to navigate by.

'Don't worry. The king has a better sense of direction than anyone I know.'

One of the nearby guards, who seemed familiar with this part of the country, added his own thoughts.

'We were well past the big headland east of Laston by the time we were attacked. With the currents coming in from the ocean, the only landfall we could make now is on the Phirmar coast. If we misjudge it, all we will have to do is row up the coast until we find the mouth of the Tonsor.'

'What about the tide?' put in another.

'True. if the tide's going out when we get near, it could make things more difficult,' conceded the first guard, 'but we're equal to it.'

The king did not seem to tire, but kept heaving his oar doughtily. When Roujeark caught glimpses of his face, he thought he could see peace there, and he was surprised. He saw his lips move in murmured prayers. Behind them five other boats were following their course. A strong wind from the south-east picked up on their right-hand side and the waves grew rougher, lifting them up and bringing them back down again. Thunder rumbled ominously in the distance, and drops of rain pattered into the boat. When the lightning started they could see that the coast was not too far ahead of them, but the rain grew heavier and chilled them. To take his mind off things, Roujeark took a turn at one of the oars, but his strokes were so clumsy that he was soon replaced and set to work with the other non-rowers bailing out the rainwater. Feeling the wind blast his soaked clothes, he suddenly regretted taking off his outer robe before the attack. With numb hands he kept bailing out water for what seemed like hours until Curillian paused in his rowing and looked round. Blowing rainwater from his face, he smiled grimly.

'Nearly there – see the coast up ahead? Those are the sandy beaches off Eithanunt; we are some way from the Tonsor. We have more work to do to reach it.'

So they kept going, following the coastline on their left. The stormy weather didn't make it any easier, and the tide was coming in, so they had to work even harder to keep from being washed onto the shore.

'Why don't we make for land?' Roujeark had to shout above the latest peal of thunder.

'Harder going on land,' shouted the guard next to him. 'We're miles from the nearest town, Eithanunt, and there's lots of fen and bog between us and Welton. We're making for the ferry-barges on the River Tonsor – they'll take us straight to the city and do all the hard work for us!' They passed a network of small river mouths, which his companion informed him was the Memitor Delta. After that they rounded a small headland. Beyond was marsh country, the outliers of a great system of deltas. Roujeark, on the starboard side, looking out to sea, thought he could see the outline of a large ship sailing away from them, barely visible in the night. When the lightning flashed again, he could see it for certain.

'What ship is that?' he asked. The others had seen it too, and the knowledgeable guard at his side answered him.

'One of the other ferries, going back to Laston. We're close.'

He spoke truly, for the next lightning strike illuminated a small river opening out amongst the fens on either side. They passed several such small waterways, but when they reached one which was wider than all the rest, they turned into it.

'Is that the Tonsor?' Roujeark asked of his neighbour, who seemed to know so much.

'Yes, one of the six great rivers of Phirmar, land of many streams. But the barges are some way upstream, where the banks are firmer.'

Lancoir's voice rose above the noise of the storm.

'The river flows against us, bend your backs. One last push.'

So it was that their little flotilla of six captured longboats entered the relative sanctuary of the Tonsor River, and battled upstream until it was nearly dawn. The sky was lightening overhead when at last, bedraggled and exhausted, they drew nigh a high wooden platform built on poles fixed into the riverbed. Armists stationed there jumped to their feet in surprise, some seizing spears, and others drawing bows. Lancoir, who was in the lead boat, stood up and hailed them.

'Ferry-armists, stand down! We are a company of armists in royal service. Lancoir, Captain of the Royal Guards, am I.'

That name was evidently well-known, and commanded immediate respect. They laid aside their weapons and hurried to help bring the boats level with the jetty. Ropes were thrown. All the while Curillian remained discreet and unidentified. One by one, the six long-boats drew alongside and their occupants disembarked. Lancoir found out which of the ferry-armists was in charge. He drew him aside.

'Your career is about to take a turn for the better. Curillian, your king, is here.' The king stepped forward, bright eyes shining from underneath the hood which hid his identity. Flabbergasted, the chief of the ferry-armists would have fallen to his knees had Lancoir not held him up. 'His Majesty has had a misfortune, and is in a hurry to reach Welton. What is your name? Arrange the passage quickly and word will be given for your promotion. Keep us waiting, and you'll be dredging the rivers for the rest of your life.' The ghost of a smile played around Lancoir's lips as he watched the alacrity with which his command was obeyed.

'Fear always gets them moving,' he remarked under his breath to the king.

'Most of the time. Love works better.' Lancoir looked at the king, expecting a rebuke, but instead saw a lesson. 'How many are we, Lancoir? Take a head-count.'

'Ninety-three, ourselves included,' Lancoir returned quickly. Curillian closed his eyes momentarily.

'Seven lost.' Just then, Surumo came up. Curillian grasped his shoulder. 'Glad to see you still with us, Commander.'

Surumo grinned wolfishly.

'Ah, wouldn't miss the next stage for anything. Your orders, sire?'

'Get the cohort to Welton as quick as may be. We will take stock there. Leave two guards behind to meet Piron and the horses when they arrive.'

Roujeark was seeing a different side to the guards. They were pale and weary, and grimmer than ever with their wounds. If only seven had perished, dozens more were wounded, and some badly so. He saw the toll that events had taken on them, and wondered what he himself looked like. How close he had come to death hadn't yet sunk in, but he was shaking with cold and fatigue. The rain was easing, but low clouds hanging over the delta and the eerie cry of seabirds made it a very uninviting place. He did not know what was supposed to happen next, but when he found himself shepherded along the platform with the others, he suddenly saw what lay behind the jetty.

The platform itself was high enough, and built sufficiently far downstream for the ferries to dock and then turn round where the river was wide enough for them to do so. Beyond the main platform were steps leading down to a lower platform lapped by the water. This soggy platform led right out into the river where a line of broad punts was drawn up. They all had strange mechanisms in their prows and chains linking them. Pilots were waiting in the sterns with long tillers in their hands. Slowly the weary cohort piled onto these new craft. Special attention, of course, was paid to the king's vessel, and Roujeark was disappointed to find himself separated from him. He raised a tired smile, though, when he saw he was in the same barge as Andil, the tall guardsman who had tried to teach him archery. His low spirits lifted when a hefty hand was clapped on his shoulder.

'Glad you made it through, Red-breeches. Not the nicest first sea-voyage for you, eh?'

'No indeed, but luckily I had stout company.' Andil snorted self-deprecatingly. The pilot of the punt overheard them and butted in. So chirpy was he that it was plain that he was well fed and had spent the night comfortably, not rowing out on the open sea.

'So they was corsair longboats I saw you lot roll up in? Thought so. What happened? Marines normally stay dry when fighting pirates.'

'Barge pilots normally stay dry when going up the river, doesn't mean they always will,' Andil retorted testily. 'As long as you've got passengers aboard who can handle a tiller you'd best watch your mouth, ferry-armist.'

The pilot spread his arms exaggeratedly wide and pouted, aggrieved. Andil and Roujeark settled down on one of the benches. After a night cramped up in the longboat it was the last thing they wanted, but there was nothing for it.

'This damn sacking doesn't do much to ease the arse,' complained Andil. 'Maybe the king got a cushion. Blasted nuisance, those rogues. Still, one thing's for sure: they won't attack a ferry again for a long time. Word will get back to the other corsair captains that an entire galleon was lost in the Dagger.' He smiled grimly, still trying to get comfortable. From his seat, Roujeark investigated the craft they were sat in, trying to understand how it worked. The pilot standing behind them was grasping a tiller, not a means of propulsion.

'There are no oars, no sails,' he said. 'What are we going to do, paddle with our hands and feet?' Andil and one or two other of their fellow-passengers laughed.

'No,' chuckled Andil, pointing forward. 'See that contraption at the front of the king's barge?' Sure enough, a sturdy metal frame dominated the bow, supporting two chunky pulleys. Wet chains were looped through them, running off into the river. 'That thing is connected to a massive winch somewhere upstream. They have water buffalo heaving on them to draw the barges upstream. When more than one barge is required, like now, they're linked together by chains and get tugged along in convoy. All they do is hitch up some more buffalo to provide the extra muscle.' Barely had he spoken and the king's boat jerked away from the platform, some hidden signal having been given.

Roujeark let the small mysteries slide by him and tried to get comfortable. His tortured back, knotted gruesomely from the cramped night, gave him little respite, and the passage up the river was hardly smooth, but it was better than it could have been. His arm stung from where the spear had grazed him, but he was not seriously hurt. Strangers to these fens on foot might wander for weeks, lost in the shifting waterways, and would be lucky to emerge alive. Uncomfortable though it was, the ingenuity and industry of Maristonia had provided a solution. As they went, they passed many other craft going both ways, and dimly Roujeark began to guess at the importance of this river as a trade artery. When they passed areas of firmer land on the banks, they saw busy quays where sea-going vessels transferred their wares onto barges able to navigate the upper reaches of the river. Timber and amphorae of wine went upstream, and sacks of grain and vases of oil went downstream. At several points, their barges pulled into one of the jetties, and Roujeark realised that no one winch and chain system could span the whole river. Again and again they disembarked the old barges and boarded new ones, making what seemed to be painfully slow progress. Andil seemed unperturbed, though. The sun, having burned off the clouds, was beaming down hotly now, and he stretched out, lapping it up.

'One of the marvels of the East-fold – never been up the river so fast before.'

Eventually, after most of a day in transit, they came to a settlement with a bridge. It was a sort of trading depot, enjoying proximity to the only bridge over the river and The Waterside Road that ran over it. Between the river, which ran from top to bottom of the Phirmar, and the road, which linked the full breadth of that same province, this was one of the three key hubs of commerce in the region. Roujeark struggled to make sense of the chaos of boats clogging the river, or of the throngs of goods and merchants on the banks, but their barges were guided soundly to this last winching station. News of the arrival of important visitors had plainly gone ahead of them because every other river-user was careful to get out of their way. A special message seemed also to have gone on before them, for a group of horses and grooms in matching livery were waiting for them at precisely the point they disembarked. Roujeark wondered how this had been arranged, but then he glanced up at the white-stone tower dominating the depot's skyline, and saw colourful processions of flags rising and falling in signals he couldn't decipher.

One of the waiting grooms addressed the king as he reached the quayside.

'Your Majesty, word reached us of your coming, and of your desire for discretion. His Grace the Duke of Welton extends his compliments and begs you to make use of these horses for your advanced party. Lodgings are already being prepared for you in the ducal palace. If you'd like to follow me…'

In the commotion of the place, few paid much notice to the grim armed company pushing their way through to the road. The king, Lancoir, and a select detachment of guards mounted up on the horses. Roujeark thought he was about to be left behind again, but to his surprise he was beckoned forward to an empty saddle. His muscles protested as he heaved himself up into the saddle, but it was better than walking. Led by the head groom, they made their way to the road. There they were met by a mounted escort of knights also bearing the livery of the Duke of Welton, the king's cousin. Straightaway they took to the road, setting a brisk pace away from the river and towards the city.

They followed a small tributary stream as it ducked under wooded slopes and wound up a hill. The road was as well-maintained as any Roujeark had ever used, which was just as well. He was fed up with being uncomfortable, and wondered if this day were ever going to end. They splashed across the stream at a ford before rejoining the road. Now it led up a steep slope. Breasting a low rise, he finally saw their destination. Welton was a great city, dominating the hill on which it sat. The white stone of its elegant skyline shone faintly in the gathering dusk. Folk going to and from the city scattered to make way as the cavalcade thundered towards the city gates. They scarcely checked their pace when entering within, and then their guide led them through well-paved streets to the most graceful building of them all. The duke's palace was a gorgeous white-stone complex with colonnaded façades and airy courtyards. Its beauty was lost on Roujeark, who was sore in every part and nodding in his saddle. He had barely noticed Welton – the largest city, after Mariston, he had ever been in – as they had clattered through it. He didn't remember when he got separated from the king's party; all he could recall was being ushered into an opulent suite and falling asleep before the door was shut.

He must have only slept for a few hours when knocking awoke him. Through bleary eyes he was astonished to find the king himself at the door.

'Roujeark, my friend, I hope you're not too tired to visit the baths?' Roujeark didn't even know what he meant, but he followed all the same. Lancoir and several of the guards were also outside, and together they were led by a servant to a warmly lit building. Inside, the air was thick with aromatic steam. Sheepishly, Roujeark allowed a servant to take his robes, and the others did likewise. He felt suddenly puny next to the chiselled bodies around him. His eyes widened when they walked into a low dome-ceilinged room dominated by a large, steaming pool. Water was running in alcoves all round the outside and in smaller pools beside the main one, where eminent-looking armists were already bathing. Roujeark had heard of aristocratic bathhouses in the south, but he marvelled to see the reality. For him growing up, a bath had been a rare occurrence, and involved plunging into a cold mountain-stream; here, it was an art form. He soon discovered why it should be housed so ingeniously, for the water was deliciously, almost unbearably, hot, and as he sank into it, he began to feel his self-consciousness seeping away. Slowly his aches and pains went with it.

For a while their group sat in silence, but then a conversation started, discussing the venture so far. It turned out this was a rare treat for the guardsmen as well, and they were soon dismissed to another corner of the bath. Curillian smiled at Roujeark's obvious bliss.

'Nice, isn't it? I fear there won't be many places like this where we're going, so enjoy it while you can.'

'It was very kind of Your Majesty to invite me here, although I was surprised to find a saddle left empty for me.'

'Roujeark, nothing has changed since we spoke by firelight under the trees, you need not trouble with titles. You're as bad as dear Lancoir here. No, this is a place for relaxation. I thought you might enjoy it rather better than the tents of the cohort back at the bridge. But I can't go inviting all my armists into my cousin's baths, now can I?' Soon after he spoke, an important-looking armist came and stood by them at the pool's side. Much younger than Curillian, there was still a resemblance between the two.

'Cousin Illyir, how nice to see you.'

'Curillian, blessed am I by this visit. Come, shall we not enjoy the steam together and talk?' The two of them went off, leaving Roujeark alone with Lancoir, who was reclining in an adjacent corner. He suddenly felt intensely conscious that he was bathing with an armist who only recently had exuded such hostility towards him. Lancoir was no longer hostile, but neither was he exactly warm. Still, Roujeark tried to glean a few answers from him.

'It is late – do you know if the king has any plans for tomorrow?'

'Plenty, but none that need get you early from your bed. Enjoy the duke's hospitality until the rest of the cohort join us.'

'I hope those we left in Laston have a safer crossing than we did.'

'They ought to. But it will be at least a day before Piron's lads join us.'

'Then what? Where do we go from here?' Lancoir gave him a funny look.

'You should know. You're the guide, after all.' Roujeark felt uncomfortable under his stare.

'I know the way from Kalimar, but to get to Kalimar I followed the Armist Road; I never came this way. This part of the country is wholly unfamiliar to me.'

'Well,' said Lancoir, apparently satisfied. 'His Majesty hinted at needing to find something out here in Welton before going on, but he hasn't told me what. Unless things take a very strange turn, we'll be riding north to the Broadsword Gap, which leads out into the open East-fold. Hopefully you'll know better than me after that…' That awkward question hung in the air until a servant-girl approached them.

'Captain Lancoir, what a pleasure to have you again,' she said coquettishly. 'Your usual?' Lancoir beamed a rare smile, and made to get out of the pool. Wrapping a towel around himself, he patted the girl playfully.

'Atellia, you and your skilled hands are the best thing about this soggy land.' Almost as an after-thought he looked down at the embarrassed Roujeark.

'Red, ever had a massage?'

Roujeark might have lost some sleep to the bathhouse visit, but the hot water and the ministrations of the masseuse had made it well worth it. Under skilled hands his knots and aches had disappeared, and now his skin shone with the oil. Exhausted, but at peace, he slid into sleep.

He was still sleeping soundly when the king rose with the dawn and set off alone into the city. Lancoir, who missed nothing, had tried to insist on going with him, but Curillian left him behind. The Captain of the Royal Guards could rest. A messenger was to be sent on ahead to Arket, and Surumo had orders to march the cohort up from the bridge depot to the barracks at the summit of Welton Hill, but nothing else needed to be done.

Curillian had deliberately dressed modestly so that he looked like an ordinary noble-armist and not like a king. He left the distinctive Sword of Maristonia behind and went with a humbler blade by his side. He liked being able to walk among his people unrecognised. It had been his practice at whiles to do so, and very rarely had any ordinary person known him for who he was. And he liked Welton, too: it was an ancient city, even more so than Mariston, and well-built. Its wide streets and beautiful buildings paid homage to the fact that elves had dwelt here long after they had forsaken the rest of Maristonia. The suburbs lower down the hill were more modern and armist-built, to accommodate a growing population, but the old citadel, here in the highest part of the city, retained the simple grandeur and curving masonry of sea-elf architecture. It was in this old part of the city that he wandered, passing the townhouses of great nobles, ancient churches and some of the city's public buildings: the library and amphitheatre. He stopped outside a lofty house. Walking up the path between peach trees, he knocked on the richly carved door. A servant admitted him, and, as expected, directed him to the top floor. It had been the same last time.

He knocked again at the door marking the end of the last flight of stairs. This time all he heard was a muffled voice within bidding him enter. It was a spacious, airy apartment, such as was beloved by rich merchants, but unlike the living quarters of well-off armists, this one was filled with extraordinary artefacts, manuscripts, decorations and hangings: the result of a lifetime's collecting. Warm sunlight and a breeze were flowing in from a wide balcony, and there he saw a lonely figure taking his ease. White-haired but fresh-skinned, the figure reclined on a couch which was positioned in the shade, but still able to look out over the city and the country beyond. Without a word Curillian occupied the empty couch next to him, and for a long time they both sat and contemplated in silence. Curillian took his time – you had to with Gerendayn. They looked out over a broad and fruitful land beneath blue skies. Sun-drenched orchards were in blossom and a sea of young corn was waving in the fields. Low hills lazed in the distance.

'The last time you came to see me,' Gerendayn began languidly, 'was when the harracks were making a nuisance of themselves. Mortals have seen nine and sixty summers since then. Dare I hope that something exciting has brought you to me now?'

Curillian looked over at the elf.

'Nothing excites you anymore, Watcher: you have lived too long and seen it all.' The tall elf smiled and stretched like a cat.

'I have been in this land since the elves first came here, many moons and suns before your people were even awake. I have watched the kings and merchants come and go. I have watched the armists take over. I have watched Welton grow old. The span of your life, deemed long by your kind who marvel at you, is like a beaker being drained next to a vat. I have…'

'I need to get to the Mountain,' Curillian interrupted him unapologetically. Gerendayn was shaken from his reminiscences and looked across at his guest, startled.

'Eh, what? What's that now? The mountain? *The* Mountain? Heh, you should be so lucky. Not even the elves remember where it is anymore. No one knows…'

'But you know,' Curillian interrupted again. Gerendayn threw out a careless arm.

'I know people who know…'

'People?'

'All right,' the elf confessed, '*a* person. A person who might not be too forthcoming at the moment.'

Immortals never are, thought Curillian. Obviously, he was wrong, years ago, to think he had aided elvendom enough to not have to play these knowledge games.

'What's your business at the Mountain, anyway?'

'Kulothiel is holding a tournament, as you well know. Just like you knew I'd be coming here, so you can drop the act. I've got a young fellow with me who says he been there, and whom Prélan wants to get back there, but he only knows a route through Lithan's backyard. How do I convince Lithan to let me pass? Sooner or later, one of you undying fogies is going to tell me something useful.' Gerendayn gasped in mock outrage.

'The cheek of youth! I was one of the obliging souls who elected to accept your long-sires as kings of this land, and this is all the thanks I get? Asking is cheating, O king. It is a tournament, after all.' Curillian smiled and helped himself to a date from the nearby bowl.

'What's the good of a tournament if no one can get there? Lithan's hardly going to let us stroll through and hunt around right under his nose. And even if I opted for stealth, accompanied by just a few, even *I* couldn't sneak past without him knowing,' Curillian explained.

'It's not any old tournament, you see. Quite a carrot the old Keeper's dangling, I hear. Who've you got with you, apart from this boy?'

'Lancoir, and a cohort of my guards,' Curillian answered.

'Only one Knight of Thainen? You are confident, aren't you? Where are the other eleven?'

'The usual. They're either with my ambassadors in foreign courts, or overseeing the frontiers. There was no time to collect them, and my realm is safer behind me with them guarding it. But if this is a game,' he went on, 'then the world is the board and all the things in it are pieces. You're one piece, and I just happened to get to you first. How do I get to the Mountain without offending His Immortal Majesty?' Gerendayn sniffed daintily and ate a date himself.

'So you need a way to keep Lithan happy? You may be in luck. There may be a service you could render him which would make it impossible for him to refuse you. This person I mentioned…'

'What person?' demanded Curillian. 'Do I know them?'

'I should say so. You saved each other's lives once or twice while gallivanting around in Lancearon's little empire. She might need you to again.' Curillian had long ago learnt not to take this elf's irreverence seriously, and so he took no offence at his labours being alluded to so lightly. Instead he thought about who he meant.

'*Carea*.' He breathed the name. Enchanting encounters from centuries ago flashed through his mind.

'Carea,' confirmed Gerendayn. And then, because he could not resist relating news, he spilled over into sudden loquacity. 'Yes, you remember her, don't you? The radiant daughter of Therendir, she who is one of the oldest, and one of the loveliest, creatures on this planet? The untouchable, shape-shifting princess of the forest, the spell-weaver and heart-breaker extraordinaire? Spurned the advances of just about every eligible wood-elf prince in the land, yet somehow found your tedious company compelling. Goodness knows what the two of you really got up to in those adventures, but I do hope all the tales are true.' He paused long enough to grin mischievously. 'But of course, they don't make songs about *those* parts, do they? Certainly not in the courtrooms of Maristonia. But if you went to the forest realm, now, well you'd hear some delightful yarns there…' Curillian jogged his digressing train of thought and steered him back on track.

'Where do I find her? You said she might not be too forthcoming at the moment?' Gerendayn sighed.

'There are some, armist king, who wouldn't thank me for getting her mixed up with you again. Last time she did that she fair near got herself killed, and you can thank Prélan that never happened, otherwise you'd have had every wood-elf bachelor from all the world's forests after your blood. Then again, she may be in worse trouble now. Her father, Prélan bless him, long ago gave up trying to predict what she'd do next, but he must be worrying his undying beard grey thinking about this latest fix. Always the rebellious child. To think that such single-minded stubbornness could reside within such serene fabulousness…'

'Trouble – what trouble is she in?'

Gerendayn looked remorseful for a moment, as if weighing

whether he'd said too much, but then his love of a listener won over again.

'Strewth, you don't want much do you? Find me the Mountain! Get me in Lithan's good books! Give me the name! Tell me the trouble! No one in the land knows what trouble she's in – one day she's a hawk, the next a deer, the next only the canniest wood-elf there ever was. Do you have any idea how hard it is to keep track of a girl like that through fen and fold, fell and forest?'

'Of course not,' said Curillian, 'but I reckon she tells you more than anyone else. You two have some way of communicating. Only not many suspect it other than me.'

'Well, if you will press me. Word from the wind is that she's fallen foul of the harracks.'

'Harracks?' said Curillian, amazed and alarmed. Gerendayn gave his most serious face.

'Yes, harracks. Nice symmetry, isn't it? It was those blighters brought you to me last time. Goodness only knows how she managed to get snared by the stone-huggers, but somehow she did, and now she's probably holed up somewhere in Faudunum. Get her out of there and Lithan will be in your debt. Never mind safe passage to your little tournament, half his kingdom wouldn't be too big a reward for you...'

Faudunum, thought Curillian. The city of the harracks. Hidden in the Black Mountains, it was a remote and mysterious hive of evil. He had been there before, and didn't relish the thought of returning. He stood up and ventured out into the sunshine, rubbing his arms. The mere thought of it had made him feel rather cold. Gerendayn had subsided into quietness again, tinged with sadness. His jollity had parted to reveal the anxiety beneath.

'Well,' announced Curillian, getting up. 'I suppose I'd better go and pay my respects to Dácariel, hadn't I?' He had nearly walked past Gerendayn when the old elf shot out a hand and seized his arm. When he looked down, he saw desperately worried eyes looking back up at him.

'You will rescue her, won't you Curillian?'

Curillian smiled reassuringly and detached himself gently. He patted the elf's shoulder. 'Don't worry, Watcher, I'll save your muse.'

V

By Way of the Broadsword

ROUJEARK gazed up forlornly at the map on the wall. Built out of tessellated stones of many colours, it depicted a portion of the world centred on the East-fold of Maristonia. It extended far enough west to show Mariston, and far enough east to show most of Kalimar. The teaching of his father meant he knew more or less what he was looking at. Yet when he tried to trace his journey to Oron Amular, he met with only confusion. He couldn't fit the pictures in his memory to the thick dark humps showing the mountains of Kalimar. He had been happy enough today, wandering about the palace and discovering some of its charms and wonders. The scholar in him had happily passed a few hours in the duke's archive, where dust filtered through the sunbeams. He had got his boots mended, and whilst waiting he had heard Lancoir and some of the others hard at work, sparring in the training yard. Some considerate soul had even laid out clean clothes for him. They fitted well enough, and they even matched his old colours, only not so faded. Yet now he had come to a disconsolate impasse. The king might have played down the difficulties of getting through Kalimar, but Roujeark still felt keenly a sense of responsibility for the path finding, and couldn't help but imagine what Lancoir and the guards would think if he came up empty-handed. They would think he was a fraud, wouldn't they?

'Are you all right? What is the matter?' A sweet voice spoke behind him, and he turned round to see a little armist-girl behind him. She wore the beautiful dress of a noble-born child, and spoke with the confidence of aristocracy.

'Well, no,' he crouched down to confide in her. 'You see, I don't know where I'm going.' In a gesture that took him aback completely, she reached out and touched his cheek.

'Don't worry. If Prélan wants you to be somewhere, he will show you the way.' He stared, amazed, into the soft brown eyes, thinking that instead of a young girl he was speaking with an angel. He was only persuaded that he was not when the girl's mother appeared at one of the arched entrances and called her daughter to her. She smiled kindly at the stranger, but took her daughter away in her arms. The child waved, and Roujeark, still stunned, waved back. He reverently touched fingers to his cheek, feeling as though Prélan Himself had touched him.

He was in much happier spirits at the meal that evening, but still shy amid so many lofty and well-born people. In another gesture of generosity, the king had obtained an invite for him to the duke's table, and now he ate well with the duke's household, albeit at one of the lower benches. Lancoir had spent the day like a caged tiger in the palace, unleashing some frustration by hacking at a stump in the palace's training ring – the sounds of which Roujeark had heard from the archive. The guards had been much happier to take their ease, chatting to the servant girls of the palace. No one knew where the king had been, but now he was back he was merrily enjoying the company of his family. Duke Illyir had responsibility for ruling the entire East-fold in the king's name, answerable only to his cousin. He held forth merrily over his meat, but asked no questions about

Curillian's quest. If he asked after every venture of his restless cousin, he would never stop asking.

The next day, Curillian summoned his companions to him and took his leave of the Duke of Welton. On horseback again, they left the citadel by a small postern-gate and crossed the head of the little valley, which ran down to meet the Tonsor where the bridge stood. Roujeark was pleased to find that they did not journey long, only up the slope behind the city to a small fort. Partially hidden by cypress and cedar trees, it looked down over Welton and the valley. It was manned by a small garrison, but inside the place was full, for the King's Cohort was there. They were greeted upon arrival not only by Surumo, but also by Piron, who had arrived the previous night. So the twenty left behind to mind the horses had re-joined their comrades. Save for the seven who had died at sea, they were all together again. Curillian went in search of Theamace, his horse, and left Lancoir to remind everyone that they were to depart the following morning.

The guards of the cohort spent the morning getting their gear ready. Extensive provisions had been laid on by Duke Illyir, along with some more unusual items. Curillian had requested spike-studded mountain boots, thick clothing, gloves and small picks. The cohort still did not know what their mission was, but as they packed the new equipment it became evident to them that mountain-climbing would be involved. What the mountaineering paraphernalia suggested, the long coils of rope for each guard confirmed. Questions were directed at Surumo and Lancoir, but neither let on anything, saying only that all would be revealed in due time. To divert the restless troops, Piron took them on a training run. Roujeark managed to escape that sentence, but he was soon enrolled by members of the fort's normal garrison to help them feed and groom the cohort's horses. Later they were taken for exercise too, to strengthen the limbs which had been cooped up aboard ship.

It was not until after the evening meal that Curillian called his followers together and addressed them. The guards were sitting around several fires in the courtyard, polishing off lamb and chicken and roasted vegetables from long spits. They licked their fingers as the king stood on the wall-steps. He was dressed in a white tunic, whose golden embroidery twinkled in the firelight.

'My Royal Guards,' he called, raising his voice above the sound of many conversations dying away. 'I trust you've enjoyed the trip so far? I can now reveal that we are bound for Kalimar.' He paused to let the round of surprised remarks run their course. 'You are my escort to a rather unusual gathering of many nations. More than that at this stage I will not say, but to satisfy the curious among you our next step will be northwards. You do not have long left amidst the comforts of the fat East-fold, so enjoy them while you can. Before long, we will be leaving our horses behind and climbing into the mountains. That is where our friend Roujeark comes in. He has a unique knowledge of our final destination, and so he will guide us. Although he is not one of you, I expect you all to treat him as if he were. Get some good rest. We leave at daybreak.'

Roujeark was conscious of many eyes on him when the king disappeared, going to hold conference with Lancoir and Surumo. The guards around him broke into excited chatter about the king's revelation, and many theories and suggestions were put forward as to their destination. None came close, though. Some of them plied Roujeark with extra food and more wine, but although he accepted the comradely gestures, he gave nothing away. When he went to sleep, he was aware of being the subject of many hushed conversations. He had aroused fascination before. In the uplands near his home many communities had debated, over many tankards of ale, the identity and purpose of the wandering conjuror who had visited them, but now he had the feeling of being involved in something big.

In the morning, their cavalcade left the fort just as dawn was colouring the sky. Watched by the garrison, their horses carefully picked their way down the steep slope at the back of the hill, which led down to the Tonsor again, and then splashed across the river using a ford. The washerwomen of a nearby village watched the large mounted company in astonishment, and so too did their husbands and brothers from the fields: such a warlike party was very rare so far from the road. Once across the river, they rode across gently sloping ground, skirting every now and then the tilled fields of settlements. In the distance to their left rose the hills which gave birth to rivers like the Tonsor. Roujeark had learned from the map in the duke's palace that high ridges like that ringed the Phirmar, completely fencing it in. Outside, to the north, lay the East-fold proper, where Roujeark had journeyed before. Beyond the southern fence, though, lay Swordhilt Peninsula, wild lands stalked by primitive tribes, which had never been subdued by Maristonia.

Scarcely a sign of life did they see all day: Curillian was deliberately leading a path which avoided the local villages. At the end of the day they crossed another river and made camp soon after by the banks of one of its tributaries. Roujeark sought out the king's company and attached himself to the royal campfire.

'What river is this?' he asked the king when he got a chance.

'The Wellain, the greatest river of the Phirmar. He's the older brother of Tonsor, and almost half as long again in his course. Follow its bank downstream and you'll come to Welham at the throbbing heart of the Phirmar: the second city and port of the region.'

Curious, Roujeark asked another question.

'And what is our next immediate destination?'

'Arket – we'll meet some friends there.'

Roujeark remembered Arket – a busy and prosperous market town that he'd passed through on his first journey to Oron Amular. Roujeark was still curious, but no more specific questions came to mind. He went to bed with a strange feeling of unease.

As they rode the next day, the uneasy feeling grew on him. Following the stream up its course, he noticed the land start to close in around them: they were leaving the flat plains and entering into a bottleneck between two of the ridges. Almost without realising it, Roujeark found that he had followed an advanced party out ahead of the rest. Apparently his subconscious desire to be close to the king had made him keep pace when the king and Theamace rode ahead with a dozen of his guards. Curillian, who knew the land better than any of them, acted as scout at the front with one other. The rest of them followed. They had to be careful riding now, for the land became difficult and broken. Lots of dips and hillocks rippled the landscape, and boulders of increasing size obstructed their path. Roujeark's feeling of unease redoubled, and he looked about for some cause of it. They had ridden into a defile now, a deep crease in the land which was filled with yellow gorse and great boulders fallen from the rock faces above. He scanned the stony walls on either side.

The right-hand lip seemed to glow with a faint red colour. Roujeark blinked to make sure he wasn't seeing things, but when he reopened them the tinge was still there, even though no one else had seen or remarked on it. His skin prickled with a memory of its own, and he remembered his strange sensation right before the pirate ship had appeared in Dagger's Cove. Back then, he had discerned a warning, like a blur on the horizon, before anyone else was aware. Was it the same now? Was someone lurking beyond the rim above them?

Encouraged by the successful prediction he had made the last time, he called out to the king, his voice ringing in the ravine. The spear came crashing down like a lightning bolt. It stood quivering in the earth where it had fallen. It was quite unlike the spears Roujeark had seen among the soldiery of Maristonia: painted red, hung with golden tassel-threads, and coming to a broad, leaf-shaped point. It might have impaled the king between the shoulder-blades, but Roujeark's cry had brought him up fast in the blink of an eye. Ageless reflexes had brought his horse up fast and the spear flashed down in front of the beast's nose. The king's hidden armour remained untested. Theamace and all the other horses skittered in fright, ears twitching. What happened next, though, far exceeded Roujeark's faint suspicion.

Dark figures suddenly appeared all along the rim of the ravine, thirty, forty, fifty. Maybe the first spear had not been aimed to kill, and had been only a warning shot, after all, for a second, similarly directed weapon crashed to the ground behind the last horse of the scouting party. Hemmed in by spears and ravine-walls, the mounted armists were trapped. The ambushers had chosen their spot well: the rock-littered ground made it impossible for them to spur their horses and make a dash for it, even if they could have evaded more spears. Staring upwards, Roujeark could not tell whether the assailants were barbaric armists or savage men. They brandished decorated spears identical to those which had been thrown, and seemed everywhere to drip with red and gold. Short, ornate bows were also in evidence. They were eerily silent, making no move. The king sat fearlessly on his horse, gazing up. Slowly, resolutely, emphatically, he drew the Sword of Maristonia.

'TAKE COVER!' yelled Roujeark, somehow knowing what would happen next. Even before the shout had finished leaving his lips his legs were in action, kicking out of stirrups and propelling him sideways. The whole scouting party leaped from their steeds and crashed among the rocks beneath and beside them. Almost in the same instant a volley of weapons hailed down after them, spears and arrows. The king was the slowest to move, not because speed had suddenly failed him, but because he trusted his weapon. DRING. DRING. DRANG. The arrows aimed at him bounced back harmlessly off the Sword of Maristonia's broad blade. Curillian covered himself expertly, his hands knowing exactly where the weapon needed to be. His horse, however, had no such defence: Theamace reared high and screamed in agony as two arrows pierced his chest. Another arrow and a spear cut into him. Just before he fell, Curillian freed his legs and jumped clear. Theamace crashed in ruin and thrashed about as he lay amongst the rocks. Half of the other horses had died instantly, and two guards as well. The other guards, bruised and jarred, had made it to some sort of cover, but the remaining horses were left exposed. Some reared up where they were, and others tried to pick a hurried route of escape, but all were cut down mercilessly by the next volley.

'SAVAGES!' cried Piron, who had been with the party. 'BOWS!'

His troops knew exactly what to do, and as soon as the order was given, their bows were seized from their back-straps and brought to hand. Arrows followed quickly and then they began their answering fire. They sent half a dozen shafts buzzing upwards: a feeble reply, but at least a pair of savages were caught in the open. Their gaudy corpses tumbled noisily down into the ravine. Yet their comrades kept up such a successful covering-fire that the armist archers' next chances to fire were few and far between. The guards hid behind their boulders, unable to do anything other than keep out of the way and loose off the odd retaliatory shot. Curillian looked up at the cliff behind him: it was a good job their enemies were only on one side of the ravine's top, for if they had been on the other side as well there would have been no cover. They would all have been dead already. Chainmail might deflect indirect hits, but nothing else, and without their full plate armour their limbs, throats and heads were all unprotected.

Roujeark did his best to hide, but felt horribly conspicuous. The guards' green and grey garb might blend in amid the rocks and grass, but his red and brown certainly did not. He felt sure more arrows were coming his way than they were going anywhere else. They snapped and cracked on the rock in front of him, and he winced every time they came close. The sound of metal striking rock was like the deft touches of a master mason's chisel: CRACK, SNAP, CRACK. Flakes of broken rock flew through the air, grazing and blinding. Roujeark's nerves were being shredded. But anger boiled up inside him, too – anger at being attacked and anger at feeling helpless. Without thinking, his hands stretched up towards the attackers. His brow furrowed as he concentrated on he knew not what. His whole body shook. His hands shook too, but they also started to glow ominously. Mysterious thoughts and unintelligible words screeched across his mind, defying comprehension.

All of a sudden, his hand exploded into flame. But his hand did not catch alight. Instead, a small ball of fire sprang forth. It hurtled upwards and smote the ravine's side. A heartbeat later a second fireball leapt from his other hand. Unable to understand what was happening to him, let alone control it, Roujeark felt like a detached observer as more fireballs careered off into the sky, each growing larger and more furious. The first had not reached the savages – smashing the rock-face beneath them instead – but the last couple exploded on the rim. Shards of rock were thrown up in a deadly hail of splinters and garish robes caught fire. Several of the savages caught alight and danced along the rim, screeching in helpless pain. Somewhere in the distance, faint and remote, a horn blew, but Roujeark barely heard it. The momentum of the power coursing through him had thrown him off balance and now flaming missiles were exploding just in front of him. Somehow, he managed to wrench back control of himself, and he collapsed back behind the boulder, panting and smouldering.

Through the smoke and charred boulders he became aware of the guards gaping at him in astonishment, and not a little fear. He himself was too shaken to move, let alone tap into whatever resource had just welled up within in, and try and use it in a more controlled manner. Scenes from his childhood flashed before his eyes and he quite forgot the scene around him.

Curillian was no less amazed than his companions when the fireballs started leaving Roujeark, but he at least had seen such missiles before. They had been a stock-weapon of the warrior-wizards in the Second War of Kurundar, deadly and practically inextinguishable. Even now, as if fed by some otherworldly fuel, the flames licked around Roujeark's boulder, despite having precious little to burn. Such a display had not been seen for four hundred years, and yet here it was, unexpected, uncalled for, but more than welcome. When the fireworks ended there followed a brief respite in which the terrified ambushers tried to get hold of themselves. Taking courage from their numbers, they soon resumed their rain of arrows and spears. But it was not so dense this time. Before long Curillian noticed them thinning out. Were they running out of projectiles, or were they despairing of destroying their victims this way? Whatever the reason, Curillian's seasoned instincts told him that if the enemy did not retire, they would soon be coming down. He gripped his sword-handle, determined to make them pay. He saw that the sheer wall of the opposite cliff had been blasted away by some of the misdirected fireballs, and what was left was a gentler, if still steep, slope, leading down into the defile. Sure enough, the foreign raiders began to slide and scramble down the new slant, intent on pressing home their attack. They came on with scimitars and spears, howling and yammering.

Curillian, King of Maristonia, rose to meet them. Leaving his cover, sword-first, he closed with them. An arrow smote his breast but fell back, turned by his impenetrable armour. A spear was flung, but he ducked away from it almost contemptuously. The lead savage never had time to even deviate from his course before Curillian cut him down. Several others sought to take advantage of the momentary distraction and hack at the king, but when their blades came scything down, they met only thin air. He was no longer there. He had moved on, quicker than their minds, and was now beside them. With the speed of a striking snake, his sword sliced through the neck of one of them, came cleanly round, and ripped open the belly of the next. He booted that savage to the ground, where he laying writhing in his own entrails, and lashed his pommel-stone backwards into the jaw of the next savage who sprang toward him. Deftly Curillian righted the blade and split open the skull of the enemy who had crept up behind him. The savage whose jaw he had smashed was still trying to recover his balance when Curillian ran him through. Barely ten seconds had passed and five savages lay dead.

By this time, Piron and the other guards had barely broken cover. As they rushed into the fray in support of their king more horns sounded, closer this time. Not nearly so lethal as the king, but still deadly enough, the guards dropped their bows and went to work with their swords and daggers. Now they made their attackers pay for their cowardly ambush, slaying without quarter. But the enemy was resourceful. It took them less than a minute to start shying away from normal hand-to-hand combat and resort to other techniques instead. Swift and agile, they used the boulders like launching pads and flew through the air to jump down on their enemies from above. In this way several of the guards were brought down. Some of them never rose again, their throats cut as they lay dazed; others grappled their opponents on the ground, rolling and punching, heaving and battering with loose rocks.

Roujeark all the while hid trembling behind his boulder, clamping down on his smarting hands and biting his lip. Every now and then he twisted to glance out at the fight. He saw swords rise and fall; red-clad savages propel themselves through the air, figures wrestling desperately. He saw one guard cleave a savage completely in two with one mighty sweep of his two-handed sword. As the shorn halves fell away like butchers' shanks, the guard swung the sword free and raised it high for another blow. But as he did so, a two-footed kick caught him in the sternum and sent him crashing down. Unable to retrieve his sword in time, the savage who had felled him sawed his scimitar across his face and chest. Roujeark shrank away in horror. Terror suffused him and he was suddenly forced to confront death. Was this where their adventure ended? Even though the king was still fighting, unscathed, surely they would all die here. With his next panicking glance, he saw another two guards fall: one with a rock-blow to the face, the other's legs hacked from beneath him.

Concern for his companions wrenched Roujeark out of his shock and he began to focus again, striving in his mind for the magical formulae which had so recently clicked within him. Nothing came, only pricks of fear lancing through his concentration. But then he heard a mighty sound.

'MAAARISTONNNNNNN!'

An instant later. a warrior came leaping through the air, sword brandished. Leaping off one of the boulders, just as the savages as done, Lancoir jumped into the battle with a blood-curdling war-cry. He was still in mid-air when a chorus of horns blared somewhere close by, filling the narrow space and shaking the loose rocks on the blasted wall. Each of Lancoir's outstretched boots connected with a savage, and he crashed to the ground, taking both of them with him. Lurching up, he attacked first one, then the other, and slew them both with fearsome strokes. Drawing breath, he yelled again.

'MARISTONNN!!'

The cry echoed in the ravine, and instantaneously answering cries came back as the main body of the guards came rushing into the fight. The savages, who had been exulting in the slaughter of their quarry, now looked up in dismay. They fled from the oncoming armists, and then remembered that the most dangerous armist of all was still behind them, unconquered. They saw the dozen bodies piled around the armist with the great sword, and their courage deserted them. They dashed for the steep slope which led back up to their ambush site. The guards were hard on their heels, and they would never have made it, struggling up the loose earth, had their comrades lingering above not thrown down ropes to rescue them. Seizing hold of them, or jumping over one another to clutch at them, they were hauled and dragged upwards. Surumo, now on the spot and organising his troops, targeted them with archers, and though they scored one or two hits, the majority escaped over the ravine's rim and out of sight. Scorning to ask for mercy, the few left on the ravine's floor were slain by the vengeful armists.

Roujeark emerged from hiding to peek over the top of his boulder, and looked out over a dreadful scene. Ten of the guards lay dead or horribly wounded. Piron, bleeding prodigiously, and one other were the only survivors from the advanced party. Curillian carried not even a scratch, but he wept as he walked amongst the gore. Roujeark watched lines of blood drip down more than one boulder. Tears poured from his own eyes as he counted the grey-green bodies amid the red-clad corpses.

The wounded were carried out of the defile and a camp was set up not far ahead on a low hill. A detail of guards was left behind to pile the enemy dead and burn them. Then they bore their fallen comrades, together with their weapons, in honour from the ravine. They were cleaned and tended and laid out on the grass of the hill. Roujeark learned that they would be borne to Arket for a proper burial, of the highest honours.

'We saw the explosions,' Lancoir told the king quietly as they stood over the slain. 'You hadn't ridden on that far...and yet just too far. Would that I could have arrived sooner.' Stolid as any, he shook like a leaf as he tried to contain the rage which blazed within him. Later, in a calmer mood, he would learn how Roujeark had fought them with the fireballs of wizards, and he was amazed. But for now, as he stood shaking, a single tear coursed through the layer of grime on his cheek.

Songs of death and mourning were sung by the guards over their fallen companions, and the wounds of the injured were tended to. Piron had been hacked deeply in his side. His right leg was gashed from knee to ankle, and three fingers were missing from his right hand, cut from where they grasped the rock as he fell. Andil had put an arrow through the eye of his mutilator, and it was Andil who now cleaned and bandaged his hurts. The only other survivor had a bandage wrapped around his head and a dozen other cruel cuts staunched, but no healing could come to the traumatised face and stupefied eyes. His mind had been skewed by the blow to his head, and his friends wept bitterly to see this proud warrior reduced to such a pitiable state. The rest of his life would be spent as a harrowed invalid in an army hospital.

Curillian turned to Lancoir, and his voice grated with anger.

'Take forty guards. Hunt those scum down. We will go no further until every last one of them is dead.'

Even Lancoir blanched from the king's anger, but he hurried to do his bidding. He hand-picked those he wanted to take with him. The chosen forty shed everything that would encumber them, taking only weapons and water-gourds. Lancoir tightened the vambraces on his arms and gave his detachment terse instructions. Swift and grim, they filed out of the camp on their vengeful mission.

The remainder of the cohort – sixty-three royal guards – stayed in the camp, resting. Over and over in his mind Roujeark tried to reconstruct what had happened to him in the defile, but all his efforts failed him. In the end he gave up trying and tried to rest his strangely weary mind. A lethargy came over him so that he dozed the afternoon away and didn't rise again until the sky was blood-red with a brooding sunset. The soldiers around him were quietly getting on with their various duties with a subdued air, but Roujeark saw the king standing at the edge of the camp, outlined against the ruddy sky. His back was to the camp, and he was looking out at the world, hands clasped behind him. He remained like that until night had fallen and an improvised evening meal was being doled out. Roujeark was again feeling uneasy, restless. There had been no word or sound of the hunting party, and worries played around the fringes of his mind. Suddenly the king called a guard to him and gave some instructions. Whatever he said was not positive, for all were grim-faced as the orders were relayed and soldiers criss-crossed the camp. Roujeark saw that the sentry positions around the camp were being strengthened and expanded.

He got up and approached the king. No obvious worry showed in the king's face, but it was tight and grim-set.

'I was just about to suggest a stronger watch myself, but then I saw you were already doing it.' He felt impertinent, giving advice to so veteran a warrior, but the king gave him a solemn sideways look.

'Concerns have been in my mind, too. You seem to sense danger long before anyone else, Roujeark.'

'Maybe I have been lucky,' Roujeark suggested.

'There is no such thing as luck. Every small feeling, every tingle of the spine, is part of a Prélan-given instinct.' He paused. 'Is it for us that you fear, or the hunting party?'

'I'm not sure. Possibly for the hunting party,' Roujeark mused aloud, 'but then again, maybe for us.'

They fell into silence and studied the night together. The camp had grown quieter as a nervous mood settled in. Pans and dishes were left neglected as taut senses strained. The horses sensed their masters' anxiety, pacing and whickering nervously. The night itself seemed to grow quieter, eerily so. Soon all that could be heard was the gentle crackling of watch-fires and the occasional hoot of an owl somewhere in the blackness. Eager to help, but knowing of nothing that he could do, Roujeark just watched and listened. He was just about to retire, thinking his vigil was in vain, when the king stirred almost imperceptibly beside him. Roujeark watched his hand fall to the sword-hilt at his side, and felt his own tension screw up tighter. A few nerve-jangling moments passed and the king made no further sign, but then, very slowly, he bent his knees into a combat stance, and pulled the sword a few inches out of its scabbard.

Open-mouthed, Roujeark watched as the sword swept out and back in an elegant arc, its brilliant blade catching the firelight like a mirror. As it swung through the air with a whistling scythe, the darkness in front of them smudged and a dim figure came leaping through the air. A split second later the accompanying howl registered in Roujeark's ears. The sword and the figure met in mid-air, and the sword won. It clove right through the leaping head and brought the body behind it crashing to the earth. The tell-tale jewellery and bright red garments had been removed, but it was still undeniably one of the savages from before who now lay prone before them. Curillian, who had been unwilling to let the enemy know that he had spotted them, now yelled a war-cry to alert his comrades.

'MARISTON!'

Those who hadn't seen him prepare his deadly greeting, like Roujeark, certainly heard the cry, and weapons were brandished. All around the camp, figures suddenly came leaping out of the dark, howling their hatred. They had rubbed mud on their faces and hands and dirtied their bronze spear-blades and arrowheads, and had thus managed to creep up on the armist camp unawares. Only Curillian's long-honed instincts had detected them. The defenders were momentarily dazed; their night-vision was spoilt by gazing at firelight, and they were on the back foot straight away. The sentries were hard-pressed in desperate hand-to-hand fighting. Horses neighed and whinnied in fear as they heard the sounds of metal striking metal.

Roujeark looked around in rising panic. He saw the confused shadows of dozens of mini-battles raging in the firelight. There seemed to be hundreds of the enemy, scores of them drawn like moths to each watch-fire. The armists must have been outnumbered three or four to one. Unarmed, he had rushed within the rapidly formed defensive cordon, and now watched from inside like the injured. He watched the king fend off the enemies near him. He alone seemed unfazed by the darkness. He moved and fought with the fluidity of a warrior whose prowess derives from innate ability rather than drilled lessons. The Sword of Maristonia burned like a brand, catching and rejoicing in the firelight with every sweep and thrust. Roujeark thought he actually saw sparks fly as other weapons came into contact with it and were shorn away.

A cry behind him made him turn around and he saw one furtive attacker who had slipped through the defensive ring. He watched the line of his movement and saw that he was making for the wounded, who sat or lay huddled in the centre of the camp. With a speed that surprised even him, Roujeark rushed to where a guard's bow and quiver lay abandoned on the ground. With no more practice under his belt than a few pop-shots loosed at the pirates from the ferry, he notched an arrow and let fly. The attacking savage had closed to within a few feet of the wounded Piron when Roujeark's arrow plunged into his belly and threw him back. Piron shot him a grateful look.

Meanwhile the battle still raged, and Roujeark longed for something more that he could do. He couldn't shoot from inside the cordon, for fear of hitting the defenders by mistake. He took up a burning brand from one of the fires and held it aloft. Without command or focused thought, he felt the same onrush of intuitive knowledge that had come to him earlier. Raging formulas and flashing lights seared inside his head and his hands glowed again. This time it was so intense that it was painful, and he could only watch, stunned, as the flames of the brand shot upwards in a great jet of fire. Like a towering beacon the flames leapt into the sky, instantly illuminating the whole hillock. Where before only shadows and reflections could be seen, now garish firelight revealed the scene in harrowing clarity. It lasted only moments, though, for the pain in his mind grew and grew until it became unbearable. In agony he dropped the brand and slumped unconscious to the ground. The brand extinguished and lay smoking beside him.

Both defenders and attackers alike had been startled into abeyance by the sudden light, but when it faded, they fell upon each other again. They barely heard the war-cries in the distance coming rapidly nearer. Some of the less wounded who were near Piron rushed to help the fallen Roujeark, and so it was that they never saw the return of Lancoir. Along a huge segment of the fighting ring, the attackers were taken in the rear as the hunting party came to the succour of their comrades. Battle-fury glinted in Lancoir's eyes as he cut down a pair of savages, screaming aloud.

'MARISTONNN!!!'

With equal relish, his picked hunters slew the unsuspecting enemies and in an instant turned the tide of the battle. Having freed one side of the hillock, they rushed round to the other sides where their comrades were still beset. Only slowly did the savages become aware of the new threat, and many of them were cut down where they stood by avenging swords materialising out of the night. As realisation gradually dawned that their night-attack had failed, they started to slip away. Soon the few survivors were in headlong retreat into the night. One or two of the guardsmen tried their luck shooting into the night, but they were rewarded with only a handful of hits.

Blood-spattered but beaming, Curillian and Lancoir met on the battlefield and embraced, still holding their swords.

'Two timely appearances in one day, Captain of the Guard – anyone would think you did it by intention!' Lancoir flashed a rare, wolfish smile.

'The day hasn't come yet when my king is attacked and I don't get a say.' He proffered his blood-rinsed sword in evidence.

Together they strode to the centre of the camp and the sight of Roujeark lying prone, surrounded by worried guards, immediately drew their concern. Their fears abated when he was roused just as they came up. He looked pale and exhausted. He moaned, and when he rubbed his head, they saw that his hands were scorched and his robes singed. Curillian squatted beside him and laid a hand on his shoulder.

'Roujeark, my friend, what is wrong?'

At first, the wide eyes didn't seem to register the sight of him, but then they focused and a look of alertness crept back into the face.

'My king, forgive me for failing you…blinding light, scorching heat…' Curillian shook his head in amazement at the wholly unnecessary apology.

A faint voice spoke up nearby.

'He seized a brand from the fire, as if to see the battle better. But then he transformed it into a pillar of blazing light. I thought all hell was about to break loose, but then he shrieked in agony and fell down like a stone.' It was Piron, telling of what he'd seen.

Lancoir nodded and came to squat on the other side of Roujeark. Like the king, he laid a reassuring hand on his quivering shoulders.

'We'd hunted fruitlessly for hours before we came upon a small group of them, guarding all their booty and bright red cloaks. It wasn't much of a fight, but we realised the main body was out on a hunt of its own. We were part-way back when we saw the pillar of fire. Then we came at a sprint. Prélan only knows how many more of us would have died had we not seen that sign. You didn't fail, Roujeark. You did well.'

VI
Whispers from the Wood

ROUJEARK was in such a daze that he didn't even realise it when they reached Arket. Between throbbing pain, weariness and bewilderment at his experiences, he only just had the energy to remain in his saddle on the ride. He had been oblivious when they emerged from the higher ground on either side and left the Phirmar behind. He hadn't noticed the openness of the new country or the long, gentle slope leading down into that vast, shallow depression known as 'The Bowl'. Dominating the East-fold, The Bowl boasted some of the best arable land in the realm. Skirting its rim was the Armist Road, which ran between Mariston and Kalimar, and this they now joined, riding eastward. Even though Roujeark had trodden that road once before on his previous journey, he didn't register that he was now retracing his steps. Now that they had left the empty, half-wild lands behind and returned to civilisation, they passed through many market towns lying on the road, and shared the road with many people travelling between the towns. Roujeark took in none of it.

Arket was larger than most of the other settlements on the road, being, after Markest and Aldia, the largest town in the East-fold. With its encircling wall – a relic of old troubles – it was more of a city than a town, but the wall was not in good repair, and the gates had been enlarged to allow for better trade access. Its gates were not even closed at night. Threats did still exist in this part of the realm – bandits and harracks in the wilderness to the north, savages beyond the hills to the south – but Arket was so well protected by the legion stationed nearby that its walls were merely decorative. The 15th Legion, commanded by General Horuistan, one of five legions making up the Eastern Army of Maristonia, was garrisoned in permanent camps strung between the great road and the rugged highlands to the south. Well-maintained pickets, forts and watchtowers kept the commerce of the East-fold secure. General Horuistan was usually so busy patrolling these facilities that he rarely came to Arket, and kept no permanent residence there, but having received the message from the capital, he made sure he was in the city in time to meet his king.

The burgesses and guild-masters that ran the city were much perturbed to find a meeting taking place between the king and a general, both rare visitors to the city, in their Guildhall. Curillian reassured the anxious businessmen and sent them away. Lancoir watched silently from the edge of the room as the king gave the general his orders. Curillian did not share many of the details, but told Horuistan to carry on holding exercises and maintain a state of readiness until informed otherwise. The meeting was short and sharp, and the general soon left to return to his command headquarters. Curillian and Lancoir together walked through the city towards the home of one of the city's dignitaries, whose hospitality they had imposed upon.

'He was surly,' remarked Lancoir, who had never met Horuistan before.

'Yes,' agreed Curillian. 'Horuistan is one of a breed of capable but over-comfortable generals who keep our peace-time army ticking over. I believe he feels aggrieved at having been passed over for promotion to Constable of the East-fold. He may be the oldest and longest-serving officer in the Eastern Army, but I am not in the habit of rewarding the unremarkable. He will serve his purpose, though, and with luck, won't be needed at all.'

'That fussy, mouse-like fellow didn't seem too pleased to see us either.' Curillian smiled at the description.

'The President of the Municipal Council, you mean? He's cooperative enough, but I'm sure he'd very much like us to clear off as soon as possible. He needn't worry; we won't disrupt his careful routines for very long.'

They arrived at their destination. The armist who'd found himself playing host was the Master of the Grain-guild, one of the most important officials in the area.

'A delight to have you here, Your Majesty,' he kept saying over their roast beef and wine. 'And, of course, what a privilege to entertain one of the valiant Knights of Thainen,' he added on several occasions. 'An honour to make your acquaintance, Sir Lancoir.' The portly armist, who seemed to have a somewhat story-book notion of soldiering, far from being put out at the sudden obligation, seemed rather taken with his guests. 'We don't get many visits from heroes like yourself out this way. Even His Majesty is a rare guest. Though, if I may say so, Your Majesty as often appears out of the blue mid-way through some adventure, as he does on official state visits, with his court in attendance.'

Lucky for you, Curillian thought as he sipped his wine. I expect you wouldn't want to waste too much of this best Redmar vintage on my courtiers. To entertain my full royal court would strain even the resources of someone as wealthy as yourself. But Curillian did not voice these thoughts. He was quite used to mildly impertinent remarks about the eccentricities of his kingship. Instead, he responded politely.

'I'm sorry to have given you so little notice, but it is very kind of you to put us up. It is so much nicer to keep up with important subjects than to hide away in one of my villas, or in an abbey.'

The dinner and the conversation ran its staid course until a steward came in with a message for the Master. The otherwise impeccable armist seemed in a state of some distress.

'Your Eminence, a crowd of ruffians has arrived at the door, and demands an audience with His Majesty.'

Lancoir hastily rose and pulled off his napkin. 'By your leave, sire, I will deal with this. Your Eminence,' he nodded curtly to the Master and left the room.

Some of the anxiety of the steward seemed to have transferred to the host. With a worried expression on his fleshy features, he leaned towards Curillian.

'We're not expecting any trouble I hope, are we, Your Majesty? I'm sure Sir Lancoir has the matter in hand, but might I enquire who these people are?'

Curillian smiled disarmingly. 'It's quite all right. I have contracted the services of some specialists for a particular task. It is nothing to cause you any alarm.'

'Ah, I see. And will they, er, be staying the night?'

'They will be making their own arrangements, and will be no bother at all to you.' The anxiety left the Master's face. 'In fact, we will all be gone by morning, so as not to indispose you any more than necessary.'

Quite recovered to his normal dignified self, the Master concealed his relief rapidly.

'So soon? I am sad to learn that I cannot enjoy any more of Your Majesty's company. I shall by the envy of the Council just to have had this encounter. Still, I must say that I'm glad to have your reassurance that everything is in order. You see, as long as the right grain gets on the right waggons, as long as the right amount of bread gets baked and the urbanites are kept are happy, I may be said to have done my duty. I really don't go in for anything else, and must confess to having no experience whatsoever of more, er, exciting matters. It is just marvellous to have had an opportunity to assist Your Majesty.'

The 'ruffians' were waiting for the king in the stables of the Guildmaster's mansion. There were ten of them. Ruggedly dressed in hooded cloaks and sturdy well-worn boots, they were sufficiently unkempt and sported enough unusual weaponry to alarm any comfortable city-dweller. Surreptitious yet confident, they exuded an intensity that only the inexperienced could mistake for unscrupulousness or hostility. However, only the most trained of eyes would be able to spot the marks of insignia about their persons. These marks were all that remained of their uniforms. Crested rings, tattoos, subtle devices woven into their dark clothing, each marked them as belonging to one or other of the Eastern Army's five legions. Scouts, trackers, pathfinders, hunters, they were highly specialised legionaries whose attire and equipment was tailored to their role.

'Gentlemen, glad you could make it,' Curillian welcomed them. He greeted several of them by name, having worked with them on previous enterprises. Lancoir had brought them round to the most inconspicuous part of the mansion, away from prying eyes. 'I'm sure friend Lancoir here has briefed you on the basics already.' They nodded confirmation. 'Now we've got representatives here of all five legions, yes?'

'That's right, sire, two of us from each,' said one. 'The rest are waiting outside the walls. We didn't want to attract too much attention.'

'Good. I need to know how many of you have been to Kalimar, and I'm especially interested in those who've been through the Black Mountains. I want those armists to meet me at the royal hunting lodge, half a day's ride downslope of Hearthel. I will be there in a day's time, so see that they get there before me. Messages have already been sent to arrange for provisions to be made ready there. Now I realise I've asked for quite a specialised group, but there's work for the rest of you. Lancoir?' The Captain of the Guard stepped forward and handed sealed scrolls to a representative from each legion. 'Three cohorts to scour Broadsword Ridge and the lower Saneth to identify the routes of heathen incursions. They will then co-operate with the 17th at Welham to flush out any threats. The remainder should keep themselves in readiness in the vicinity of the 15th's barracks – General Horuistan may have need of you. He is aware of your availability, and will deploy you as and when needed.'

'Questions?' barked Lancoir. As was to be expected from such capable armists, there were none. Curillian cocked a quizzical eyebrow when one of the trackers, a seasoned old campaigner, cleared his throat.

'Not a question, sire, just a comment. A pleasure to be of service to you again. It's been too long since we had a proper job to do.'

Roujeark slept through all of the meetings and planning. All he knew in the morning was that he was being turfed out of bed before it was light and ushered through a hasty sequence of breakfast, toilet and packing. Before he was properly awake, he was in the saddle again. Seemingly only a score of guards were currently with him – he didn't even know where he'd spent the night – but soon their group was joined by others emerging out of the shadows. If he hadn't been riding alongside Andil he would have felt thoroughly disorientated. Gradually the King's Cohort coalesced and by the time they reached the city's eastern gate, with only the merest suggestion of predawn light in the sky ahead of them, they were all together again. They left Arket before even the early-rising market traders and stallholders were about, and townsfolk who thought they'd been disturbed by the massed hooves of a mounted company assumed they'd had a bad dream.

With unusual speed, they thundered along the road as if straining against a pressing deadline. Wretchedly uncomfortable, Roujeark rode in their midst. Fresh air whistling past his face and the beauty of dawn unfolding in the open sky had brought him more fully awake. To his surprise he found that his burnt hands had been salved and bandaged whilst he slept, so that he was just about able to control his reins, but they were still raw and painful. They must have covered a good many miles at their breakneck pace, for the normally busy road was still virtually deserted, when, without warning, they changed direction and turned off the road, plunging into the open country to the north. Once off the road they slowed down, as if some danger had now passed, or possibly also because the lightly wooded land through which they now rode was less easy going than the neatly paved highway. Roujeark, who had originally thought himself the expert guide, was fast abandoning the notion as he found that travelling with the King's Cohort was simply a matter of trying to keep up while trying to guess the king's mind. Thankfully they had now slowed down enough for him to fire a couple of questions at Andil. Their brief conversation was punctuated by numerous ducks, swerves and jolts and the scream of disturbed birds as they cantered downhill through scrubby heathland.

'What was all the rush this morning – the sun's only rising now – and why have we left the road? Isn't that the quickest way to Kalimar?'

'Orders,' Andil replied tersely. To Roujeark's immense gratitude, he went on to elaborate. 'It seems the king is keen to be as inconspicuous as possible. He normally travels by main roads with an entourage of thousands; this is different.'

'Why are we not all here?' asked Roujeark, whose rough headcount kept coming short.

'Some of us are still not here – they went south off the road as a diversion.'

'Why?'

'Don't ask me the ins and outs of it. But basically no one knows we're here now – we left the road before people were abroad to notice us. My guess is we're headed for one of the king's private lodges, somewhere nice and discreet. Another day or two and we'll be in Kalimar.'

Andil's guess turned out to be quite a good one. The sun was approaching its zenith when they came to a hunting hall. Far off the beaten track, it lay in a clearing in a large wood. Roujeark was alarmed to see mounted armists waiting for them outside the hall, but evidently the king was unperturbed. The reeve who maintained the royal property was clearly expecting to see them, for no sooner had they been spotted than vast amounts of provisions were arranged on the patio outside the hall. The king disappointed Roujeark's hope of having a quick word by immediately vanishing inside the hall with the resident servants, so the young armist found himself enrolled in helping to transfer the victuals to the horses of the cohort. Loaves of bread, bags of flour, flitches of salted and cured meats, packets of nuts and dried fruit, wedges of cheese and linen-wrapped cakes and biscuits, gourds of wine, skins of water, flagons of cider, there was enough here to sustain an army. Bewildered, Roujeark wondered what the onlooking horses thought of this soon-to-be doubling of their loads. While he helped, a gang of the horsemen who had been waiting for them here accosted him.

'Look here, lads, I didn't know the king's cohorts rode with mascots these days.'

'Cor, will you look at this fellow? Not conspicuous at all is he? I don't mind these other fellers, they'll blend in at a pinch, but this one's asking for trouble.'

'Stick out like a sore thumb he will, spot him a league off.'

'He'll get himself shot right enough.'

'Shot?' said Roujeark, alarmed. 'By whom?'

'Elves?' suggested one of them helpfully. The voice was behind him, and Roujeark turned to face him, the other armist fierce but smiling happily. 'Savages? Harracks? Bandits?' he went on cheerfully.

Roujeark turned again when the original speaker gripped his shoulder. Shocked, he found the armist was almost nose-to-nose with him, all aggression and hostility.

'Who knows?' he said, his deep voice grating. 'Maybe they'll all have a go. Seriously though, is this some kind of joke?' Roujeark winced under the heat of his enmity and recoiled from the stale cider on his breath.

'Soldier!' A stern voice made the pugnacious armist step away. Roujeark noticed, with surprise, that it was Piron who was intervening. The armist who had accosted Roujeark clearly held a rank of his own, but he did not pick a fight with the officer. Reducing his animosity to a restrained malevolence, he listened respectfully to the guards' officer.

'You'd do well not to make an enemy of the king's friend. After watching him incinerate more than a few savages, I'd be doubly careful. Now, get your people in order.'

'Incinerate, is it?' the armist muttered. 'Interesting.' Eyeing Roujeark curiously, he moved on, and one of those with him gave Roujeark a playful shove as he passed. Piron bit on an apple as they moved away.

'They're trackers, expert pathfinders. Some of the most skilful, and least courteous, members of the army.' Roujeark surveyed Piron and saw that his wounds had been dressed neatly, just like his own.

'I'm surprised to see you're still with us, Piron, I thought you had been too badly wounded. Surprised, but glad.' Piron shook his hand, acknowledging the kindness. 'Ordinarily I would have been, but I wasn't being left behind, was I? Nearly killed me again, but just had to show them I could keep pace. I'll be fine, provided I'm not attacked within the next few days. I believe it will be worth sticking around.'

'What do you mean?' said Roujeark.

'Well, between Lancoir's presence, the sudden emergence of a wizard in our midst, and the fact that we've been attacked twice already inside our own borders, I'd say we're in for one hell of an outing.'

'Oh, I'm not a real wizard,' said Roujeark, embarrassed and intrigued in equal measure. Piron gave him a comical look of feigned apprehension.

'By Prélan, if you're not, then I'd hate to meet a real one.' He continued to eat his apple while doing just enough to seem like he was supervising the activity about them.

'What is this place?' asked Roujeark.

'A hunting lodge of the king's. He has hundreds of them across the realm, probably doesn't visit any of them more than a couple of times a century. Curillian's not even much of a hunter, by comparison to some. He prefers to hunt enemies, not game. Guardsman Andil here will know more.' Andil strode up, happy to join the conversation.

'Don't know the place personally, but judging by the state of readiness here I'd say orders for this lot were lodged some time ago – how else could a country reeve get so much tuck assembled in time? Must have called in all the tax owing to the king in kind from the local landowners. The king's chosen a good spot, ideal as a base for operations, but nice and discreet.' Roujeark could see that Andil thought a lot more about what went on than the average member of the riding. Piron added another surmise of his own.

'We'll only be waiting until the chaps in the diversion rejoin the main party. Then we'll be off again. Any idea how the king plans to sneak into Kalimar?'

'I don't think even Lancoir knows that,' said Andil. 'No, that knowledge is for the king only, and perhaps also for our guide?'

Roujeark, however, didn't know. Having left the road, he had totally lost his bearings. He kept close to Piron and Andil as they left the following morning, riding further into The Bowl and angling slightly towards the rising sun. Roujeark didn't mind revealing his ignorance to his two friendly companions, and he gleaned everything he could from them.

'We're steering a very deliberate course,' said Andil. 'We've given a wide berth to all the busy farmland over there to the right. The town of Irlaton's probably not more than a couple of leagues upslope.' Their puzzlement grew as they rode. Presently they came to a river with a strange, greenish hue.

'That can only be one of the waters that issues from the forest,' declared Andil. Piron paled slightly.

'Surely we're not going through Tol Ankil? No armist I ever heard of has been through there and returned to tell of it.'

'Maybe the king has,' said Andil.

They followed the course of the river upstream for a time, and as they did so the banks became increasingly wooded. Up ahead, the trees appeared to get much denser. Clouds had been gathering overhead, and now a light drizzle was falling. Then they noticed Lancoir come riding back down the line. He reined in alongside them, and Surumo, sensing instructions were afoot, spurred up to meet them.

'The king sends word,' Lancoir told them, 'that there'll be a brief delay soon. Surumo, there's a confluence not far ahead. Halt the armists there. From there only a small group of us will ride forwards. Roujeark, you're wanted in the king's company.'

Roujeark shrugged and left his companions, riding up to the head of the line with Lancoir. They came to the expected confluence and then the guards, who now numbered 91, were left behind. Those who rode on with Lancoir, Roujeark and the king were the ten trackers who had joined them at the hunting lodge. Ignoring the surly glances of his newest companions, Roujeark was far more concerned about the trees ahead. Nervousness was mounting inside him, and his skin seemed to tingle as if reacting to something in the air. It was quite unlike anything he had ever experienced in Maristonia before; only his meetings with Prélan came close.

The clouds were low and the rain heavier now, giving the whole country a mysterious, uninviting feel. Roujeark started in his saddle when they suddenly rode within sight of a thick wall of trees. They had reached the forest. He had never imagined it would be so great. Even though the clouds were so low as to be almost fog-like, he got the impression that before him was a vast tract of unguessable woodland. When he had ridden into Kalimar before he had only heard rumours of the great forest near the border – it had always been just beyond the edge of sight from the road – but now the forbidding nature of it struck him. This was not a place where mortals strayed lightly. He sensed an anxiety similar to his own in his companions. Only Curillian took it in his stride, but even he was warier than normal.

Out of nowhere, an arrow sped and buried itself in the turf before the king's horse. Green-flighted and almost invisible against the backdrop, it seemed to vanish into the ground. However, the message it bore was all too clear. Horses and riders alike jolted in alarm. Even the trackers seemed taken aback. Wherever the arrow had come from, their sharply honed skills hadn't detected a nearby threat. Ahead of them the line of trees, half-hidden by the film of heavy rain, seemed to brood like a garrison enduring a siege. Unperturbed but grim-faced, the king freed his feet from his new horse's stirrups and dismounted. He entrusted the reins to Lancoir.

'I go alone from here. Do nothing until I return.' His tone brooked no argument. So Lancoir took the reins and, fidgeting in his saddle, watched anxiously as his sovereign strode ahead into the rain. There were keen eyes among them, but even from their sight he had disappeared by the time he reached the treeline, apparently without suffering harm. The trackers were grim and silent, seemingly quieted by the forest's oppressive presence. Lancoir too said nothing, straining his eyes for sign of the king. After a while, however, he sensed the futility of his vigil and relaxed a little. Roujeark edged closer, and, no louder than he dared, spoke to the Captain of the Guard.

'You care for the king a great deal, don't you?' Lancoir seemed to bridle, as if sensing an insult, but then his features softened slightly.

'He's like a father to me.' Roujeark sensed the weight of unspoken history behind those words. Fingering the ring which Lancoir had given him, he wondered if it gave him the right to pursue this conversation further. He decided to try.

'Curillian is more paternal than I thought a king could be. I would give much to have a father figure like that. My own father was taken from me when I was a small boy.' The words were true, though he hadn't planned them. Although he had walked the world for many years and learnt much of its ways, Roujeark still felt young and vulnerable, somehow conscious of an incomplete upbringing. Lancoir did not speak for so long that Roujeark thought he would not respond, that he would not be interested, but eventually he asked gruffly,

'What happened to your father?'

'He was slain by the folk we lived near. He tried to help them, but they did not appreciate the practice of magic.' Lancoir narrowed his eyes at the mention of the word, but his expression became more interested.

'My father was murdered too,' he said at length, confiding almost reluctantly. Roujeark had to coax more out, for nothing else came freely.

'What happened to him?'

Slowly, stiffly, Lancoir conveyed his story. Had the trackers been any closer, he probably would have stifled it, but they had spread out, trying to keep busy while not actually doing anything. Rain dripped from the knight's hood as he spoke.

'He was a Knight of Thainen, just like I am now. Sir Lorumon of Markest. He was one of the greatest warriors in the land, but unlike most of the Order, he came from humble roots. He served the king well, but well-born armists around him, craven and weak, were jealous of his status, his fame. Driven by the devil, they brought false charges and evidence against him. The king took no action, but the conspirators took the law into their own hands. Ambushing my father on the road, they executed him and left his body to rot. We never recovered it. The king paid them in their own coin and executed all the known conspirators, and denied them burial honours, but I am convinced that some of them still live. There is nothing I can do to bring justice down on them, but justice will find them sooner or later. As for me, I always keep a blade by me when I sleep. They didn't want my father to be a knight. Nor me. Nor my son, Lancaro. He will be a knight after me, when he comes of age. But every day that I am a knight, and a good knight, I pour burning coals on their heads. They will never stop me being who I am meant to be.' He paused and gave Roujeark a direct look from beneath his hood. 'Never let anyone stop you from being who you were meant to be.'

Curillian walked across the wet grass, feeling the eyes on him the whole way. His boots pressed deeply into the turf with every step. The great sword was by his side, but he spread his arms wide in token of peace. Soon, he knew, he would be hidden from the sight of his companions. He hoped he would not have to leave them in the dark for too long. The trees grew nearer and nearer. He passed under their eaves. The boughs and foliage were so dense that the precipitation slackened almost instantly to a pattering trickle. Above the earthy scent of damp loam, the odour of strange plants wafted into his nostrils. Droplets of rain ran down his neck. All he could hear was birdsong in the trees. When a greeting didn't come, he called aloud to the trees.

'We've been through this before. You can show yourself.' His voice echoed under the thick canopy. Long after the last echoes had died away, the whisper came, like an utterance of the trees themselves.

'And every time you come, you fail to appreciate how fortunate you are to tread here at all.'

Curillian responded in kind.

'And if you didn't want me here, I wouldn't have been allowed to come.'

Silence. Only the sounds of the forest and the rain. He shivered and felt his skin twitching. Was that the flapping of a bird's wings? He had been expecting it, but the grey form which suddenly appeared beside him still made him start. Tall and slim as a young tree, cloaked in invisible grey, the wood-elf turned his head and only then was his pale face visible beneath the damp hood. Unreadable brown eyes transfixed him. Of all elves that he had ever had dealings with, the wood-elves, Firnai, were the most secretive, the most alien.

'So, Falakai king, you are here. The fear of the wood keeps all mortals away, but not so the doughty son of Mirkan, protégé of Lancearon, scion of ancient chieftains. Your troop did well to halt where the arrow checked them, else they would all have died without a trace ever reaching mortal lands. We knew of your coming, and of your number.'

'Our riding was secret and known to few. Are we expected? We took great care...' The brown eyes were implacable, as was the face, which hadn't moved at all, save the lips.

'Not careful enough. Your folk, who look only to the ground, may not have marked your passing, but we who also inhabit the skies were well aware of your movement. Did you hope to creep across the border undetected? Even the Avatar in their stone houses would have been aware of you. We are aware of all, even the passing of your red companion, forty years ago in the mortal reckoning. Even as now, it was early springtime when he vanished into Avamar. No, Curillian, son of Mirkan, son of Arimaya, we knew of your coming.'

Curillian looked at him, allowing a slight smile to play on his lips. *You don't know why I'm here, though, do you?* He scrutinised the face next to his, and realised he knew it, though it had taken two minutes for the recollection to come back to him. Sin-Solar, or was it his twin brother, Sin-Tolor? The great yew bow hidden by his side was the mighty emblem of both, and their sister too, inescapable marksmen and guardians of the forest all. Did the princes often stand sentry in these latter days, or had other word reached them?

'Gerendayn,' he said, searching for a reaction. There was none whatsoever. 'Has Gerendayn sent word from Welton? I know he has the capability. You probably know the conversation I had with him word for word. Whatever else you may or may not know, you at least know I'm here to see her. Take me to the queen.'

'Come, she is near.'

The elven prince had not been exaggerating. Curillian had followed the fleeting grey figure only a few hundred yards through the trees before they came to a great fallen oak, a giant of the forest. The prince led him to the foot of the slanting trunk and gestured him up it. Pacing up the broad wooden slope, Curillian reached a point where lightning had cloven the trunk in two. He stood near the edge of one of the spars and wondered what was meant to happen next. He started when the blackbird came and hovered in front of him. It looked strangely at him for a few moments, and then it changed before his eyes. He had seen wood-elves shapeshift before, but never so close up. The surprise of it nearly knocked him off the trunk. Where before there had been a beautiful bird, now a beautiful elf-woman stood before him, dark-haired, dark-eyed, graceful with ageless elegance.

The eternally young body was only visible for a heartbeat before what had moments ago been feathers were drawn about it in a dark cloak, swathing her like a robe. His mind shot back to another elf-woman, to another glimpse, in another life. Then he forced himself to focus. He knew this face, too. Eyes like dark opals, but as penetrating as arrowheads, gazed out at him from pale, angular features that were hawk-like in their beauty. The top of the black cloak was drawn up in a tall collar which framed her imperious visage. He stepped back and bowed low.

Here was Dácariel, Queen of Tol Ankil, daughter of woodland kings. So alike was she to her aunt, Carea, that Curillian thought it was she, and had to fight against being transported back to long ago days. He blushed, knowing she read his thoughts.

'Welcome, Curillian, King of Maristonia,' she said. Her voice was tough as oak roots, and yet as free and as light as wind through the trees. In wood-elven song, all the textures of the forest were given vocal form.

'Lady of the Forest, hail Dácariel, daughter of Carion.'

'Twice met are we,' said she, still maintaining an aloof regality, and then suddenly smiling like a tree in blossom. 'Far too seldom for those who have been neighbours down the long centuries.'

'I am honoured by your friendship, Lady, but I am just a sapling in the grove next to your ancient evergreen. How small a chapter in your life have been the four hundred years of our acquaintance?'

'And yet we have been comrades-in-arms in that time, an honour you have bestowed upon many of my kin. Great is that bond…nearly as great as love.' She gave him a direct look, and he lost himself in those eyes. And she was the younger, and less potent of the two… 'You have come for her, have you not?'

All the horses reared and Roujeark nearly fell from his saddle. Lancoir's sword came singing to his hand, but the cloaked figure that had suddenly materialised before them made no move of attack. Without so much as looking up or showing his face, he spoke, beckoning them.

'Come. My queen bids you join your king as her guest. You and all your company.'

The King's Cohort was brought up to the forest eaves and there they were met by Curillian, damp, but unharmed.

'Lancoir,' he said happily, 'pass the word. Leave the horses and baggage here, they will be brought after. We have been offered alternative transportation.' He saw the look in his captain's eye and added, 'Have no fear. We are welcome guests. Let there be no doubting heart, we are here as a necessary part of our quest. Come, enter under the eaves where few mortals have been and gone in peace.'

Presently a group of wood-elves materialised beside them and took charge of their mounts. If Lancoir and the officers were surprised, the trackers and ordinary guards were practically goggle-eyed – most of them had genuinely believed elves to be myths of a legendary past. Now here they were, taking their reins and gesturing kindly to them. Once shorn of all their baggage, they were led off on foot into the trees by one of the elves. As they went, Roujeark looked back over his shoulder to where the horses were disappearing in the opposite direction. He started, thinking that he had seen one of the elves leading them suddenly change into a horse herself. It had been but a brief, leaf-obscured glimpse, and a heartbeat later the whole herd had vanished with hardly a hoof-beat to be heard. He turned back, certain his eyes were playing tricks on him, and followed his comrades through the dripping trees.

After a while they began to descend into a wooded valley, which led them to a swift river. Rafts were waiting down by the riverbank, and they were ferried across the fast-moving water by tall cloaked elves wielding long poles in skilful strokes. No sooner had they disembarked than they were led up a damp slope, back down the other side and to the banks of a sister river. More craft were waiting beside this bank, but this time they were more like a cross between log-boats and coracles. They piled into these boats, surprised to find that there were enough to accommodate them all, and took up the leaf-shaped paddles. Curillian looked in surprise at Sin-Solar, their guide.

'What, are we going to paddle the eighty leagues to Firnon against the Sachill?'

'No,' said the saturnine elf. 'Since you are our guests, Sachill herself will bear us. Tell your followers to put aside the paddles.' The guide then got into the lead boat and from the prow leaned down to the river. Dipping a paddle into the current, its blade pointing upriver, he whispered a few flowing words over it. The river seemed almost to shudder in response. Then he adopted a trance-like posture in the prow, from which he did not emerge for a long time. The guards in each boat were treated to an eerie sensation when, as soon as they were all aboard, the boats started to inch out into the current as if of their own volition. At first the current started to tug it downstream, but then it held fast, as if kept in place by a restraining hand. Astonished and fearful, the guards gripped the boats' sides and eyed the water suspiciously. Then, one by one, the boats started to move off upstream, against the current.

'What is happening?' Roujeark asked the king, whispering lest he offend the sentinel elf, who shared their boat along with Lancoir and four others. Curillian smiled.

'As one who is gifted in magic, you should be telling me that. It is the spirits of the water. According to the wood-elves, every waterway, from the smallest stream to the mightiest river, has its own spirits, and they are friendly to the elves. The elves are very careful to keep running waters pure and unpolluted. Some say the spirits are the living tears of Prélan; others that they were handmaidens among his angels who were sent to Astrom to steward the waters; which it is, the elves do not tell the armists. A river like the Sachill might have hundreds of spirits, or possibly one great one. See?' He pointed. 'They glint in the water.'

Roujeark looked over the boat's edge into the river, and there he saw, to his amazement, flashes in the water. They looked like the glinting of fishes' scales, only they all pulled in one direction, not deviating from side to side. Captivated, he watched them ripple and wriggle. He trailed a hand over the edge, wanting to touch the water, but as his bandaged fingertips came close, they started to feel heat and resistance. Hastily he withdrew. He contented himself with watching the gradually changing scenery on the banks. Slowly the trees changed from the oaks, horse chestnuts and sycamores common in the East-fold to less typical species. Elms, birches and beeches started to predominate. They were normal at first, but then they started to diversify into strange shapes and varieties Roujeark had never seen before. Willows lined the bank the whole way along, but the further they went, the larger and more luxuriant they became. Were they throwing out their limbs further across the river, or was the river shrinking? A confluence came and went, and then suddenly the valley became steeper. Gradually upward they travelled, but no slackening did they notice in their pace. As they climbed into the higher recesses of the valley the trees started to change again, as the deciduous lowland species gave way to higher-dwelling conifers, cypresses and firs.

Above them the rain stopped, and as evening drew on the sky cleared to reveal the early stars. Some while later they were travelling by starlight, which danced and flashed upon their ethereal conveyances. Quite at odds with the fresh evening air, a strange drowsiness started to come over Roujeark, and seemingly over his companions too. Occasionally Roujeark thought he saw lights shining faintly in the distance in the trees, but with sleep creeping over him, his tired eyes couldn't be sure. Then he thought he heard soft singing in the trees, and it lulled him to sleep.

So smooth was their going that nothing disturbed his nodding until he was thoroughly asleep. He only came awake when a hand shook him by the shoulder. He opened his eyes to see the king looking at him.

'Wake up, we're here.' Roujeark rubbed his eyes.

'We're where?'

'Our destination. Welcome to eighty leagues deeper into Tol Ankil than you'll ever likely come again.' As Roujeark unsteadily exited the craft on to a finely manicured landing-bank, he tried to get his sleepy mind around the king's statement.

'Eighty leagues? How long have I been sleeping?'

'Not long, but your snores scared the magical fish away,' a guard said helpfully.

'We were travelling for less than a day,' said Curillian, starting to follow after the guide, who had not said a single word throughout the voyage.

'No wonder news travels fast in the forest,' Roujeark overheard Lancoir say. 'I wish we'd known about this last time.' Roujeark wondered what last time was.

'You don't know the half of it,' the king told his captain.

They had come to a sheltered bay created by a wide sweep of the river, which was much narrower here. The boats were stowed in subtle niches cut into the bank, and then they were led up a steep slope. Before them rose a steep hill, about whose waist the river ran. And around them were the most marvellous trees Roujeark had ever seen, broad-boled and impossibly tall. The trees were widely spaced, and in between them wood-elves were living out their daily lives. Some were washing clothes, some were weaving baskets or fashioning strange garments; others sat about in groups, talking or playing instruments of wood and wind. They seemed barely to notice the company of armists suddenly come into their world – they just carried on as normal. Roujeark gaped at them, never having seen anything like it. In a community of armists you might see one or two fair people, and every so often a real beauty; here, every elf was fair to behold, and many of them had a beauty that was rich and striking. No signs were there here of the dirt, disease and disorder which marred the existences he had known. It was not until they saw elves entering and exiting out of doorways set into tree-trunks that they understood that their dwellings were in the trees themselves. Looking up, they saw windows, platforms, treetop walkways and stairways.

Like many of the guards, Piron was wandering about as if in a daze. The very ground on which they walked seemed to whisper and laugh, and in the air above, vast colonies of all kinds of birds seemed to thrive. The trees themselves seemed alive, quivering and vigilant. The movement of their limbs and boughs was like a music in the forest, accompanied by the lyres, harps and pipes of the wood-elves. The atmosphere was peaceful, but it was close and seemed inexplicably stuffy, like a cosy, fire-warmed living-room. The air was filled with fragrance, sweet but so heady that it seemed to catch in their throats.

'Why have we come here?' Piron asked, his voice strangely muffled.

'To help, and be helped,' Curillian told him succinctly. Loosening the cloak at his neck, Curillian followed Sin-Solar up the slope, treading a path only faintly discernible from the grass on either side. As they passed through the wood-elf dwellings, Roujeark had the odd feeling that the elves didn't even know they were here, that it was actually some kind of waking vision of the past. He hurried to fall into step beside the king.

'How long has it been since our kind came here?'

'Guess.'

'A thousand years?'

'No. Never.' Roujeark looked at him in amazement. 'The Firnai have dwelt here unchanged for nine thousand years, since the early days of the First Chapter, millennia before our species even awoke... And in all that time, no foreigner has ever come here. Until now...'

Roujeark's mind span. In treading here with mortal feet, they were creating history. He drank in the sights, sounds and smells of this virginal encounter, but then a slightly unsettling thought announced itself to his brain. If the wood-elves' isolation was so rigid, what had happened to make them break the habit of eternity?

As they went on up the path, they left behind the wood-elf dwellings like armist suburbs. Up ahead of them loomed a hedge, a living wall. From beyond it rose up towering trees of mountainous height, a city-like cluster of green and brown columns. No guards or sentinels could be seen, but watchful eyes tracked them as they approached. Two enormous intertwined holly-trees formed a gateway by breaking the hedge and arching over the path. Once within the hedge, they seemed to enter into another world, another era. As they stepped over the threshold, everything seemed to slow down. The closeness and drowsiness of the atmosphere redoubled, but at the same time their senses heightened to report stimuli they had never before been conscious of. They had to crane their necks to look up at the trees, whose mighty summits joined together in a living vault. In the branches above them flitted birds of marvellous colours that none of them had ever seen before. Under this enormous canopy everything on the ground was thrown into shade, illuminated only by some startling radiance deeper within, while above them a thousand lamps lit the sky. Cast in shadows, the great trunks of the trees made it seem like they were trespassing in some primordial temple of titans. Many arm-spans wide and as high as towers, the armists were utterly dwarfed and cowed by these forest-giants.

Sin-Solar, seeming to glide over the grass, led them into the centre of the city, where stood a ring of the greatest trees yet. Twenty metres wide at the base and over a hundred high, it seemed impossible that they could have sprung from the same earth which elsewhere nurtured normal trees. And yet not just huge were they, but graceful and artistic also. Vast, arched limbs of trunks were flung out and enchanting patterns were drawn in living wood. Carven thrones, stalwart towers, leaping arches, mysterious recesses, spiralled boles and gossamer curtains; every conceivable type of feature was represented here in this natural architecture. It was as if all the trees they had ever seen were just essays in some fantastic art which was here mastered in a pinnacle of sculpted finesse.

At the summit of the hill, a flat crown was occupied by a great fountain, the source of whose copious waters could not be guessed. Every one of its many tiers and springs were lit by crystal lamps, so the water flashed and scattered liquid radiance far and wide.

Around the fountain the colossal trees grew in a large circle. In between each pair of trees gurgled a rivulet sprung from the fountain.

Discrete pathways led from the fountain to ornate doors at the foot of each tree. Suddenly, at Sin-Solar's gesture, they were made aware of a deputation emerging from the tree at the northern edge of the circle. The cohort crowded past the fountain and watched, awestruck, as the king went to meet the elves and bowed to them. Unlike the folk outside the hedge who had been dressed in modest green and brown, these three elves were clad in silver-grey, like the smooth bark of a venerable old beech. In the luminescence of the fountain they seemed to shimmer like apparitions. Many of the cohort could not endure the sight for long, and others backed away from the fountain, fearing what effect splashes of its waters might have on them. To allay their fears, Curillian came back to them.

'My friends, welcome to Firnon, the city of the forest. This is as far as you can come. You have already come further than any mortals before you, and from here I must go alone with one or two others. Have no fear, the Lady Dácariel, queen of this forest, has made her realm welcome to you. See, here is a servant of hers, who will guide you to quarters which have been prepared for you. There, in a little while, we shall meet again. Lancoir, Roujeark, come. Surumo,' he summoned the commander as he went past. 'We are guests here, see that my armists conduct themselves with due decorum.' Surumo nodded and led the dazed cohort in following the elf-servant off down the hill. Then Curillian, Lancoir and Roujeark were left alone. They approached the northern tree's doorway, where Sin-Solar and the two other elves stood waiting. Roujeark felt tiny standing under the tall figures, whose chests were level with his face. When he looked up into their faces, though, he saw solemn kindness and welcoming smiles. The elves turned and led them through the doorway.

Roujeark marvelled at the carving in the tree's interior, but he was not able to do so for long, as their guides led them right through the trunk and out on to a broad, balustraded walkway emerging from the opposite side of the trunk. Lit by lamps and small gems set into the handrail, the walkway instantly left the ground and led them up into the night, hugging the trunk all the way. Round and round the trunk the walkway led. Here and there it branched off to houses in the branches, or back into the trunk itself, but they continued upwards until the ground below was lost in a sylvan shadow. After a while, they realised that they had climbed so high that they were above the canopy of the forest. Enchanted, they paused on a north-facing platform and looked out over the living carpet of green. For miles and miles the trees stretched, but straight in front of them they gave way to dark slopes, and, in the distance, snow-capped peaks glimmering in the starlight.

Already giddily high, they had further to go. Their guides went on ascending tirelessly until they had led them to a wide hall perched amidst the uppermost branches. Woven screens and rich tapestries enclosed it and gave it shelter from the breeze, but they were so in keeping with the woodland colours that it seemed like a natural feature, the crown of the great tree. Little did they see, though, other than the majestic figure seated upon a raised dais. Here was the Lady of the Enchanted Forest. Many tales depicted her as a fell sorceress with her mysterious forest filled with strange servants, so the armists had heard tell of her, but the fables told in Maristonia fell far short of the reality. Beautiful and bewitching, she was dangerous and benevolent in equal measure, a mistress of many cunning arts beyond the reach of others. The elves knew her simply as Dácariel.

She sat upon a great carved throne whose arms were life-sized embodiments of stags, so lifelike that Roujeark thought they would spring at him at any moment. The dais was covered with rich green cloth and where it ended, the interwoven branches which made up the tree were interspersed with fabulous carvings depicting stags and centaurs and fawns. The whole place had a dryad charm, but there was nothing rustic about the queen herself. Dressed in a sleek robe the colour of forest berries, she wore warlike vambraces and a plumed helmet of steel. She grasped a great spear and against her throne a circular shield rested, bearing the image of a stag. No crown or adornments fit for a lady of great rank, only the martial accoutrements of a warrior queen. Ruling the largest settlement of Firnai outside of their ancestral home in the heart of Kalimar, she maintained her realm against its enemies with strength.

No less warlike were two figures standing on raised platforms around the edges of the chamber. Dressed in hunter's clothes, they held enormous yew bows which measured from throat to toe. So still were they when they entered that Roujeark thought that they were statues. He knew better when Sin-Solar, garbed and armed in similar fashion, went to take up his place on the third remaining platform. Surely these were his close kin?

It therefore fell to the other elves who had climbed the tree with them to usher them forwards.

Curillian, ar i ce Falakai, ey anionarteh maray. Curillian, king of the armists, and his companions.

The words seemed to have been spoken aloud, but they resounded in Roujeark's head like a thought. He recognised the word Curillian, but none of the others. Lancoir was no less dumbfounded than he in this surreal setting, but the king approached the dais and knelt before it. The queen arose from her throne and came towards him, speaking rich words which seemed to take wing and echo in their ears.

Graceaa Ruthion! Rol castothir lanim hánen nomille ilyadir eres marua des ton hánen. Welcome Ruthion! It makes my heart glad to have you here in my home.

Curillian kissed her outstretched hand and then rose. She stepped down from the dais, towering above him, as he made his introductions.

'This, My Lady, is Lancoir, High Captain of my Royal Guards, and Knight of the Order of Thainen.' Dácariel bowed low and spread her arms wide in acknowledgement. When she spoke, suddenly they could both hear the words properly and understand them.

'Of course, who could forget such a valiant ally of battles bygone? Welcome, Lancoir. May your strong swordarm here find rest for a time.'

'And this,' said Curillian, gesturing to the second of his companions, who hung back shyly, 'is my new friend, Roujeark.' Dácariel glided towards him, intrigued and smiling.

'Come, King of Mariston, you can do better than that.' She reached out and held Roujeark's face in a lingering caress. Her skin was warm, and her penetrating gaze made him feel like he had drunk heady wine. 'Why not say…wizard-to-be…pupil of Kulothiel…your guide to the Mountain?' Roujeark gaped at her, astonished. 'Oh, yes,' she said tenderly. 'We have heard much about you, young one; more, probably, than you have heard yourself.'

She paused, contemplating him. *So, you're the one,* he heard inside his head. His ears reported differently. 'So this is the mysterious armist wayfarer who crossed the border into Kalimar forty suns ago and then simply vanished, eluding even the best efforts of the Avatar patrols? One of such high destiny is always welcome in my court.'

She removed her hand and moved away.

'Now that we know who you are, it is only right that you should know us. Dácariel of the House of Firnar am I, queen of the woodland realm of Tol Ankil. These are my children, the guardians of my northern marches, my western marches, and my southern marches: Sin-Serin, Sin-Tolor, and Sin-Solar.' One by one they nodded their heads, but so alike were they that they could not be told apart, except one, whose face had a more feminine cast. 'They have come from their vigils in the far-flung eaves of the wood to greet you. Yet you may also find interest in the news that they bear.'

'What news, Lady?' Curillian asked.

'See for yourselves...' And suddenly a living vision was cast before their eyes, a recent memory brought to life, filling the tree-top chamber.

It was a dark evening at the edge of the forest. An armed company of men were venturing into the forest, treading warily. There was a score of them, and although they tried to be stealthy their noise spread far and wide. It was evident from their hesitant steps that they did not know where they were going, but even so they went a fair way through the trees before halting. They paused and produced axes, preparing to make a camp. The axes were only just laid against the smaller branches of the nearby trees when the arrows fell. It could not be seen where they came from, but there could be no mistaking their great number, nor the terrible accuracy with which they were fired. In the space of a few seconds, the intruders were all struck down by green-flighted arrows. Fear and shock had only just registered in the first faces as their companions fell before to a man they all lay dead, arrows protruding from eyes and necks. For a few moments all was silent, and then shadowy figures entered the scene. The vision zoomed in to show the newcomers picking among the dead bodies, investigating the fallen and retrieving their weapons. The same design was on all their hauberks, surcoats and shields: a double-headed grey falcon against a quartered green and black field.

'These are men of the Falcon Clan,' burst out Lancoir. 'They are erstwhile allies of ours.' He was shocked and angry. Curillian's face was neutral. The vision faded before them, leaving the throne-room as it had been before.

'And yet they dared to trespass in the forest, a place sacrosanct for our kindred ever since we first came here. By intruding thus, on earth forbidden to mortal feet, they invited their own deaths.' Roujeark thought it was Sin-Tolor who spoke in answer, though in truth he could not be sure. Lancoir likewise did not know which of the queen's children to face, but regardless he confronted them dauntlessly.

'So why not kill us also?' Sin-Solar stepped down from his pedestal and came close.

'You are here by special and unprecedented invite. Your king solicited permission first before bringing armed retainers within our realm. Had he not, my archers would have slain you all just like the Aranese. If they were trying to find a path to Oron Amular, they were woefully off-course, and my brother has paid them for their folly.'

'If others try, they will fare alike.' The succinct promise was uttered by Sin-Serin, the third of the queen's children, her voice barely discernible from her brothers'. Then the voice of Dácariel herself spoke again.

'All the champions and heroes of the world are abroad, responding to the call of Kulothiel. These men of the Falcon are not alone: the Hawk, the Charger, the Lion, the Unicorn, the Pegasus; all the Clans have sent contingents, and many others also. The Jeantar himself is with them. The King of Hendar rides with a strong mounted company in this direction and many of his vassals are also on the move. Courageous Ciriciens, intrepid Ithrillians, gallant Hendarians, even a dauntless warlord from the south, all are on their way. All have been seen. However they try to approach the Mountain, it will not be permitted for them to come through Tol Ankil. You alone, Curillian, friend of old, have been granted passage. For you alone have another purpose here, besides finding the Mountain.'

'What other purpose?' Roujeark piped up, his voice sounding horribly shrill and boyish in his own ears. Almost immediately he wished he hadn't spoken. All the elven eyes turned to him, before Dácariel fixed her gaze on Curillian again.

'Have you not yet told your companions, Curillian? Then let them see…' Another vision materialised in the centre of the room, so vivid and lifelike that it seemed like a world within a world.

A hooded figure was picking her way up a rough, mountainous path. It was a slender elf-woman, all alone. The wind which clutched at her cloak and sent it streaming. Even from behind was evident the striking likeness of this person to Queen Dácariel. No clue was given as to where she was going, only that her path through the stones and grass was leading her up into the mountains. Up ahead, all was dauntingly black and bleak.

None of the armist viewers were unmoved by her seeming frailty and vulnerability. Curillian's jaw trembled as he watched.

'That is enough,' he said. 'You need show no more. It is true, then? Carea is in Faudunum, in the hands of the harracks?' The vision faded at his request and the face of the queen became visible again. It was drawn and pained.

'What you have been told, you have been told aright. It is so.' Having struggled to stay silent thus far, finally Lancoir could contain himself no longer.

'What is so? Who is Carea?' Roujeark looked at him side by side with the king and saw the yawning gulf of knowledge between them. Lancoir, many hundreds of years the junior, had not had the benefit of the king's royal education and wide-ranging experience. He looked pitifully out of his depth. Even the king's customary cool suddenly seemed less assured. But Curillian did not answer. Instead, Dácariel herself answered the knight's question.

'Carea is one the oldest elves still residing on these mortal shores. She is the daughter of an ancient wood-elf king, and possessor of some of the noblest blood in existence...and she is my mother's sister. What you have just seen is the last we ourselves saw of her, walking in the direction of Faudunum, the harrack stronghold in the midst of their mountainous realm of Stonad. We doubt not that she is now their captive.' She spoke patiently, but the pain was evident in her words. Lancoir was unsympathetic though.

'And what is she to us?' he hissed sidelong to Curillian. The three elf children bridled at the disrespect, but a three-fold glance from their mother calmed them. From a mass of unspoken words, Curillian answered him tersely and calmly.

'She can help us. She alone of all those who know the location of Oron Amular might be willing to help us.'

'But what about him?' Lancoir demanded in Roujeark's direction.

'You forget yourself, Lancoir, son of Lorumon,' Dácariel said firmly. 'You are here as a guest; no one here is answerable to you. But restrain your anger for when it is needed, and perhaps you will have your questions answered.'

Curillian went first. 'Roujeark knows *a* way to Oron Amular, but it is a way we cannot use without High King Lithan's consent. Roujeark did not know that when he offered us his help – he slipped past unbeknown to anyone one – nor did I know what way he had taken when I brought him along. If we tried to rediscover his route, even two or three of us, let alone a hundred, we would be accosted by the elves of Kalimar, disarmed and escorted back to Maristonia before ever we came within thirty leagues of it.'

'Then why did you bring...' Lancoir interrupted. Curillian held up his hand and spoke over him.

'He *does* know a way, we just can't use it yet. I hope to still make use of it, but we must perform this task to be allowed to go that way. We must persuade King Lithan to permit us passage. Don't you see, dear Lancoir, that we have no other choice? If we attempt the western passes of the Black Mountains, we could wander for months without ever finding another way – the Tournament would be long finished, won by someone else, even if we lived to rue it. But to go the way that Roujeark knows, uninvited, to defy the High King, is to court disaster. Yet if we rescue one of his most beloved subjects, a kinself no less, then he would be in our debt. He would permit us to retrace Roujeark's route. And, regardless, Roujeark needs to get back to the Mountain. Whatever the problems with the route, still I would have brought him. Prélan wished it so. He spoke to me on the day we left Mariston. He wishes Roujeark to come again to Oron Amular.'

As Curillian subsided, Roujeark remembered the king speaking similar words to him by firelight in the woods. He felt again the warm glow of reassurance that he had felt then, hearing confirmation from someone else of Prélan's calling on his life.

Sin-Serin spoke for the elves.

'As for us, we do not know the way to Oron Amular any more than you do. It is not common knowledge, even among the Firnai. But in rescuing Carea, you would be putting all Elvendom, not just the High King, in your debt. Every service has its price. If you want passage, you must first rescue her.'

Lancoir was not yet placated.

'So that's it? The quest must be set aside for a mad rescue plan? Why haven't you rescued her, if she's as dear to you as you say? Has no one here remembered?' he demanded, raising his voice. 'We fought the harracks before, and the victory was as hard-won as it will prove unmatchable. Few can contend with the harracks in their own terrain. Even we who beat them never ventured deep into their domain, nor came within sight of Faudunum. If anyone has a chance there, surely it is the wood-elves and not us armists at all?'

Sin-Serin answered his question.

'Our power is in the forest; it is not in the mountains. We have learned, through bitter experience, that we are as vulnerable in the uplands as the harracks are under the trees. One of us may go with you as a guide, but that is all. The task is yours.' Lancoir was as discomfited as Roujeark had yet seen him. The knight appealed to his king.

'To challenge the harracks in Stonad, in their own back yard, is to needlessly risk the lives of the whole cohort. Better that we should go home and forget this whole business than die ignominiously in the mountains.'

'There is nothing to stop you returning to Mariston,' Dácariel told him. 'But if return you do, you will have fallen at Kulothiel's first hurdle, and others will contest the great prize without you.'

Curillian shook his head, refusing to contemplate the thought. For better or worse now, he was committed to this quest. Roujeark had listened with mingled excitement and fear in his belly, electrified at the thought that Prélan actually wanted him at Oron Amular, yet mind reeling with the thought of his current uselessness in the expedition. Scarcely thinking about what he was saying, he spoke up.

'I'm not sure what I can do, as a guide…or anything else…but whatever I can do, I am at your disposal, Lord King.' Curillian nodded and smiled faintly. He turned to look at his captain.

'I am invited to Oron Amular, and to Oron Amular I will go. I am resolved on this, and I can see no other way to ensure getting there on time and alive. Our quest depends on this. Besides, there is nothing ignominious about trying to save someone in need. I would go even if the quest were not at stake.' He looked up at the queen solemnly. 'I will go.'

Lancoir's face struggled to contain his misgivings, and Roujeark sensed the intensity burning in him. His eyes smouldered and his voice was thick with barely controlled wrath when he spoke.

'Then I, too, will go.'

Here ends The Call of the Mountain, Book I of Oron Amular. Look out for Book II: Rite of Passage, coming soon.
Read on for a sneak preview.

VII
Rock and Snow

ONCE back at the bottom of the great tree, Curillian took Lancoir and Roujeark aside before they rejoined their companions and spoke to them. The journey back down the wooden walkway had been fraught with tension and unspoken disagreement.

'I know you are not in favour of this mission, Lancoir, but I will undertake it nonetheless. I ask no armist to come with me, and no pressed armist – you least of all – will I suffer in my company. Whoever comes, we must be few. We cannot carry war into the mountains with any hope. We will neither overmaster the harracks nor lay waste their cold citadel. Rather, it is as shadows and thieves we must go. With stealth we will penetrate their stronghold and steal the captive back. Therefore, there is no risk of the casualties you fear. But make your decision swiftly: either stay here with the main cohort, or come with my volunteers.'

Curillian went straight to bed then, letting no task come between him and sleep. Lancoir instead went and reviewed his kit. Roujeark went with him, seeing him as the more likely source of answers. They joined the rest of the King's Cohort in the lodge that had been made available to them. It was a wooden structure built into a bank of earth, so discreet that you hardly noticed it until you were right outside. A carved wooden doorway gave onto a wide hallway running back into the earth. The hall was filled with a long wooden table at which the

Royal Guards reclined in shirtsleeves. In their king's absence all had evidently been washed and well-fed, judging by the aromatic steam filling the air and the well-scraped bowls littering the table. Arms and armour had been piled to one side, and some of the guard had already taken to their beds in curtained niches cut into the walls. Overhead, the ceiling was a mass of tree-roots which had somehow been twined into wonderful patterns.

The happy banter died away almost immediately as Lancoir stomped in. Fists clenched, he took in the scene with a scowl and the armists' jests died on their lips. They knew the Captain of the Guard well enough to know when he was angry. Lancoir looked as if he might speak, and the armists braced themselves, but then he stalked off down the hall. Gradually the conversations resumed once he was past, and Roujeark felt the atmosphere recover as he followed the angry captain. Lancoir went right to the far end and sought out his own gear. Roujeark watched as the captain's anger seeped out in kit slammed down, weapons slotted resoundingly into scabbards and knots tied unnecessarily tight, the rope positively whistling and cracking in his hands. Some of the guards nearby were already asleep, but one or two were wakened and made nervous by their captain's ire.

'What are harracks?' Roujeark ventured to ask at last. Lancoir continued sorting his gear, but eventually answered.

'Harracks…' he snapped, but too loud, startling several others. He fixed each with a furious glare that made them turn away and mentally block up their ears. 'Harracks,' he repeated more softly, but hardly with less venom, 'are squat little bastards who live in the mountains that spawned them. They're so at home in stone that they're practically made of the stuff. Some say they're born of the stone itself. They're tougher than dwarves, slow-moving but ridiculously hard to kill. They blunt blades and smash shields. It's like trying to fight the mountains themselves. You've probably never heard of them, because the only time they've ventured down into the lowlands they've exposed weaknesses and been beaten, but get them in the mountains, around plenty of rock, and they thrive on it like elves in trees. That's why we've never taken them on at home, nor tried to flush them out, and that's why we shouldn't be trying now.' He thumped his backpack in frustration. Roujeark could tell that eavesdropping was still going on by the way some of the prone guards nearby jumped slightly in their feigned sleep.

Lancoir gripped his bag like he was going to rip the leather apart with his bare hands, but then slowly he relaxed.

'I just don't understand why he's doing it,' he said quietly, almost to himself. He was quiet for a moment. His next words were dropped so low that Roujeark had to lean in to pick them out. 'I've seen him impulsive before, we all know his quick-fire instincts on what's right, but never have I seen him risk so much for so little reason.'

Roujeark tried to mollify his wound-up companion.

'You heard the queen, Lancoir; all the great men of the world are on the move, converging for this tournament. Do you really want to miss out on that, or not even find out what's at stake?'

The captain was silent for a long time, eyes boring holes into his pack.

'No,' he conceded, muttering at the ground. 'We should be there.' Then suddenly he reached out and seized Roujeark's tunic and growled like a bear. 'But mark my words, Roujeark, nothing this big happens without trouble. The greater the prize, the greater the price.'

Shaken, Roujeark sat on his bed watching as Lancoir rooted out some volunteers. All thought of sleep was soon forgotten.

'Right you deceitful dogs, I know you've been listening in. I know you're not asleep, so hear me now. Next bit of the mission's for a few only: I want a dozen volunteers to accompany myself and the king up into the mountains. Rescue mission. You know what's up there, so declare yourselves quick.' Roujeark felt dread creep up on him as he watched these courageous warriors daunted by this prospect. Should I be more afraid? Piron and Surumo cast their bedding aside and stood up, but Lancoir instantly snarled them down.

'Not you Piron, you're not fit. Nor you, Surumo, someone's got to keep this rabble in order till we get back.'

The rest of the guards found it far harder to find their feet. Slowly, two stood up. A few moments passed and then another two stood also, and finally two more. Eventually twelve were standing. None could conceal their fear, but none were willing to back down now. Roujeark was both encouraged and dismayed to see his friend Andil among the standers.

'Andil, Aleinus, Haroth,' Lancoir called their names. 'Cyron, Edrist, Norscinde, Utarion, Antaya, Findor, Manrion. Good armists.' He paced up and down before them. He surveyed the others, letting his gaze settle on two who were not Royal Guards. They were from the ragtag group that joined them at the royal hunting lodge. They wore different garb and had been sitting apart in a small group, yet nevertheless two of them now stood with the others.

'State your names.' Lancoir barked.

'Caréysin, sir,' said the one who was tall and slight.

'Lionenn,' said the other, not bothering to add 'sir'. He was shorter by far, but sturdier and thickly muscled. With a thick beard and mysterious marks upon his face, he was a fearsome sight to behold. Roujeark noticed a great battleaxe resting just beside him. He looked a match even for Sir Lancoir. The captain was sizing them both up.

'Lionenn, Konenaire are you?'

'Aye.'

'Been in the mountains before?'

'Once or twice.'

'Good. Keep your axe sharp.'

'Ah always do.'

Lancoir turned on the other figure.

'And you? Do you have the profession to match your name?'

'Yes sir, never missed yet.'

'Good, don't start now.'

Lancoir moved away, and Surumo spoke.

'I'll await the king's orders for the rest of the cohort.'

Lancoir nodded.

'What of the other trackers?' Surumo asked, jerking his head in the direction of a surly group further up the hall.

'We'll think of a use for them,' said Lancoir, scowling at the group. 'They know their stuff in the mountains, and more of us may yet need to cross them. Await your orders. Stay alert.' He turned back to his kit, then suddenly whirled around and barked a name. 'Aleinus,' he singled out the armist who had been the first to stand. 'Aleinus, why are you going?'

The guard in question, who looked quite young, forced a smile of bravado.

'Captain, if the king is going to fall, how glorious will be the deaths of those who fall beside Curillian, greatest of the Harolins?' Lancoir growled acceptance of that.

'Glory in death is what we all seek,' said Haroth, morbidly.

Lancoir smiled grimly.

'As so you should. But make no mistake about it: you may not know what the game is yet, but Curillian won't fall before it's all played out. The only question is how many of us will die along the way.'

Curillian allowed them a day's rest. The following day, he woke before the dawn and walked through the mists. He didn't know who his volunteers were yet, but he knew they would be ready when he was. He had one last conversation to have before he left, so he followed the shadow through the misty trees. Leaving the leafy citadel behind, he pursued the blackbird ahead of him, certain that it meant him to follow her. The bird left him some way behind, and he lost sight of it in the mists. Hurrying forward, he came to the mossy shore of one of the many lakes which dotted this northern part of the forest. There, standing on a great boulder in the shallows, the black-cloaked Dácariel stood, motionless. He joined her, walking through the water until he reached a small boulder beside the one she was standing on. She spoke practically at first.

'The easiest part of your journey is over.'

Easy? thought Curillian. I've had a ship burnt out from under me, been ambushed twice in my own realm, and many of my armists already lie dead. What does difficult look like? He voiced none of these thoughts, knowing she perceived them all too clearly.

'This seizure of Carea is not an isolated act,' she went on. 'The harracks have been very active of late, and my folk have seen them consorting with the goblins. They have given the snow-elves much trouble and even raided some of the high valleys of Kalimar itself. Together they are a great threat, and they may even attempt an invasion of the lowlands. My heart forebodes about the timing of their unrest, so close to the tournament...If you have forces nearby, it would be well to deploy them closer to the mountains, and have them closer at hand in the event of need...'

'I will do so, Lady. Those in my cohort not coming on the mission will redeploy to the foothills north of your realm, ready in case of trouble. They shall not impose on you any longer than necessary. By your leave, I have prepared orders for other units to march and join them. Indulge me and spare a guide to lead two of my messengers by the swiftest routes to the southern border – that way, word will reach my nearest legion as fast as possible. If you are in need, the Eastern Army of Maristonia will be on hand to assist you. Consider it a token of my gratitude for your hospitality.'

'It shall be done.' They fell silent for a while, and the mists enveloped them. When Dácariel spoke again, it was no longer about strategy.

'You're going to a lot of trouble, Curillian, to rescue her...' The queen left the thought hanging, neither wholly statement nor question.

'Lady, you know that I would go to her aid even if nothing else were at stake.' His voice was solemn, even though it was muffled by the mist. She turned imperceptibly towards him.

'They say that no armist and wood-elf have ever been joined in love. Yet I doubt that anyone has ever come closer than you and she.' Curillian was suddenly aware of her making intense eye-contact. 'Some thought the rumours grotesque. For myself, it only showed just how special you were, that you were able to move such a one as she in her soul. We all knew you were special, Curillian, right from when you were born. The Silver Emperor, the High King, myself, we all knew. And yet, it may be that your great deed in the judgement of history was to reclaim the throne of your forefathers after being exiled for so long; or that your greatest deeds came and went in the wars long ago. Think you that you can surpass the glory of your youth? So, I ask myself, what do you seek at this tournament? Power Unimaginable? You have already wielded great power, O King of Mariston. Glory has its limits. What makes you think that this great thing is not reserved for another?'

'There is only way to find out, Lady. I go to compete not merely for the prize, but to discover, if it may be, what Prélan's will is in all of this. My heart forebodes that this is merely the start of great and terrible things. I go also to strive for the best of myself. It has ever been so. I challenge the greatest, defy the deadliest, and strive to emulate the best and noblest. The quest for excellence has defined me.'

'No, Curillian, it has not defined you. There is no doubt that you will leave a mark on history of surpassing excellence and nobility, but those things do not define you. They are merely the symptoms of true greatness. You are, and always have been, defined by your love of Prélan, by the closeness of your relationship with Him. Verily, Prélan blesses abundantly those who walk with Him. What could you ever have achieved without His guiding, enabling Spirit? You may go and compete, O mortal king, but you must be ready, if, in this case, the will of Prélan differs from the desire of your heart. I do not ask much of you – just do as you always have done. Walk with Him. You will not fall from greatness unless you fall from Him.'

He said nothing. Staring out over the water he contemplated her words. He did not look at her when he felt her long hand caress his cheek. The hand withdrew. He heard the flutter of wings and knew that she had changed and left him.

Lancoir, Roujeark and the twelve volunteers were ready. They stood outside the lodge with their gear, and to it their wood-elf hosts had added many valuable supplies.

'Nourishing food, and warm cloaks, to help keep you alive in the mountains,' one of the elves had said. The rest of the cohort had been reunited with their horses and expected to be going again soon, but word had got round about a chosen few being taken on a special mission, and now they were disconcerted. Through the mists Roujeark could make out their worried faces. With the king still gone, none of them knew what to do next, but they did not have to wait long. Curillian came back to them, solemn and quiet. He spoke first to the officers, Surumo and Piron, calling them forward.

'My friends, with great patience you have been kept in the dark till now and asked no questions. But no longer. Up to this point, all I've told you is that we are bound for an unusual gathering in Kalimar. I can now tell you: we are bound for Oron Amular, the Mountain of High Magic.' He gave a few moments for the words to sink in and the amazement to lodge in their faces. 'Yes, Kulothiel, Keeper of the Mountain and Head of the League of Wizardry, is hosting a tournament to which all the princes and champions of Astrom have been invited. Between us, we will contest momentous prizes. Roujeark, our new friend, is bound thither, and he will be my guide. But to persuade the elven High King to grant us passage, there is a task I must perform first. That is why I venture into Stonad, the land of the harracks, now. It is a rite of passage. When I return, successful, then the main quest can resume.

'However, I do not ask you to sit here idle in a foreign place. New counsel has reached me, warning me of dangers close by and far off. The two swiftest riders, with wood-elf guides, must make haste to the southern border of the forest whence we entered and speed messages to General Horuistan of the 15th. He is to march the entire legion north and encamp between the north-western reaches of Tol Ankil and the River Amretu. You will attach the cohort to his force and be under his command, unless new orders reach you from me. Be alert, for you may well be called for before all this is over. While the messengers travel, the rest of you may take a few days' respite, but after that you must rendez-vous with the legion. On no account should any of you return into the forest, and the main legion not at all. Is that understood?'

'I have my orders, sire,' said Surumo in acknowledgement. 'For my part, I am content. I have no desire to intrude into old legends. But our swords will be sharp and ready if you need us.' They both saluted, but Piron could not hide the longing in his face.

'I would go with you, sire,' he said plaintively. Curillian clasped a hand to his shoulder, then his neck.

'I know, Piron. But you're not yet fully fit, and you need to be for this mission. Gather your strength now, for there is plenty ahead of you, great deeds and danger alike.'

Roujeark watched the king brief his two officers, watched him answer their questions, and watched him bid farewell to his cohort of guards, who were desperately sorry to be parted from him. Not many were eager to march into harrack territory, but they had come to an alien place, and were uneasy about lingering here without their king. But such was Curillian's authority that they accepted his strange decision.

Then Roujeark noticed Queen Dácariel materialising as if out of the mist itself. Swathed in her tall black cloak, and accompanied by one of her formidable offspring, she watched the farewells before gliding to Curillian's side. She spoke soft words to him that only he could hear. He looked at the queen's companion and nodded.

'Lancoir, we are ready?'

The captain gave the barest inclination of his head, his face set grim.

'Good, then let us lose no time. Sin-Serin here will accompany us, and be our guide, as her brother was before. We march to the northern border of the forest, and thence into Stonad in the mountains beyond.' The armists all bowed their heads and each in turn received the elf-queen's blessing. Then she spokc words over them together.

'...*Tûh Prélan ábécos érese livon ey allédos rol amaluph*...May Prélan smile upon your mission and grant it success.'

Sin-Serin led them along a faded and ancient path through the trees. When dawn came, it drove away the gloom and revealed a fresh and glistening forest. Droplets of water left over from soft rain in the night dripped all around. They caught the sunlight as they did so and flashed, making the leaves look as if they were made of gold. The springy grass swayed in a light breeze and vestigial shreds of mist flitted amongst the trees.

The way was long on foot, and the ground was steadily rising, but Sin-Serin marched them at a stern pace and in four days they had reached the edge of the forest. They took their leave of the sentinels at the border and found that their feet were on an ancient and faded track. As they exited from under the eaves of the forest, they saw it march uphill, away north alongside the River Pharaphir, the parent river of the Sachill.

'Ought we follow the river?' Curillian asked of Sin-Serin. 'It will surely be watched.'

The elf nodded sagely.

'There is nothing for it. It is too easy to get lost in the mountains using any other path.'

So they climbed, nervous and watchful. At first the gradient was gentle, and the river lay open beside them under the sun, glinting in the warm light. It was not as hot as Roujeark was expecting out in the open air, but he did not realise how high they had already climbed – almost the same elevation as his home in the Tribune Valley, where the fierce heat of Maristonian summers softened into alpine warmth. He enjoyed the sun but, looking up, he saw that the foothills above them were beset by glowering clouds. He shivered looking at them. Gone were the days when the uplands had positive associations for him, happy childhood memories buried beneath a layer of pain.

On the first day, their path wound in zigzags up green slopes made damp by a hundred tiny rivulets racing to join the great river below. Roujeark was a little out of practice, but he was enjoying the hike. It was obvious, though, that the guards around him, less used to trekking in the uplands, were not so happy. On the second day, the grass gradually thinned out and lost its glossy green as browner hues started to take over. Where before they had marched through miniature forests of fern, now they trudged past clumps of heather, mossy hummocks and grass-crowned stones. Down below, the unobtrusive valley sides started to close in above the river and it shrank as it flowed past steepening slopes and overhanging banks. Behind them, the forest which had seemed so vast now looked small and far off. Looking down, Roujeark felt like he stood on the ankle of a giant whose legs the trees were forbidden to touch, such was the abrupt change between forest and hillside. Again he looked up, and the crags above him flitted in and out of dark clouds like furtive titans. With increasing regularity, the sun disappeared behind clouds and swathes of shadow fell on the valley sides. The low clouds started to envelop them in an uncertain welcome. Time and again they paused to look back, but the receding forest was now only intermittently visible, peeking sometimes from behind curtains of wandering vapour.

Sin-Serin permitted them only rare and short breaks. Each time Roujeark paused, flushed with the effort of climbing, he soon became chilled and found himself piling on more clothing. Before long they were walking exclusively in clouds, condemned to dank, muted conditions. The temperature dropped alarmingly as a cold wind blew down from the mountains. It was a good thing that the king's foresight had made them well-prepared for an environment such as this. Warm layers were donned and over the top they had sheepskin coats and waxed cloaks to resist the moisture in the air.

'I'm rarely pleased to see clouds,' Roujeark overheard the king saying to Lancoir, 'but these are more than welcome – they'll hide us from unfriendly eyes.'

'For the moment...' came the guarded response.

They passed sidestreams braided with stones and caught occasional glimpses of the rocky staircases by which they had fallen into the main valley. They crossed more and more stretches of scree and loose rocks, which lay in their path like gnarled blankets casually draped across the hillsides. Ankles were turned and knees and shins were scraped. By the end of the second day, the landscape changed again. The tight valley suddenly opened up into a great U-shaped trough, flat-bottomed but walled with towering slopes fearsomely sheer.

The path, such as it was, led them past a spitting waterfall, which fell, as if from nowhere, out of an unguessed shelf above. Soon it was not just splashing falls which assaulted them with water: the damp mists in the air turned into driving rain and soaked them through. They made a sodden camp in the shelter of a low overhang of rock and conjured as good a meal as they could. The night was passed fireless and cheerless.

The morning, though, was splendid. Gone were the rains and the low clouds, and now revealed to their sight was a stunning theatre of rock. Roujeark had seen such places before, in the Carthaki Mountains. The more pious mountain-dwellers said that Prélan had scooped out the broad channels to display His majesty; the less pious were of the belief that they had been dug by giants to ease their travels. The wide valley looked like the empty hull of a rock-ship, and it stretched off into the mountains as far as they could see. Shimmering waterfalls cascaded down its flanks, gracing the sombre, rounded peaks above. Up at the rims of the valley, though, clouds lurked like distant spectators.

'Long ago,' Roujeark heard the king's voice beside him, 'when it pleased Prélan to keep the world colder, vast floods of ice gouged out these mountainous valleys like frozen warships, their broad prows snapping off all the rock that lay in their paths. In those times the world was changed, and what was once jagged became smooth.'

Roujeark listened with interest, hearing lore that was scarce heard by any outside the privileged class which could afford to attend Maristonia's universities.

'See the Pharaphir there, making its lonely way through the flat bottom of the valley? The river's all that remains of a monolith of ice – what the scholars call a glacier – which once would have soared so high as to fill this basin, right up to the rims.' Roujeark looked up at the cloudy rims, scarcely able to believe that all beneath had once been locked in ice.

'Somewhere up ahead,' the king told him as they trudged along together, 'way up in the mountains, where snow lies year-round, the Pharaphir probably still springs from a shrunken glacier, though I confess I've never seen it.'

'I've heard the tales of such places,' enthused Roujeark. 'Of high valleys where plains of ice groan like living things. And snow-folk dwell there, or so the story-tellers say...'

'Snow-folk?' Curillian laughed. 'I think they're a fairytale even to the elves.'

They would have continued to wander, marvelling, through that mighty open-air cavern, but Sin-Serin took them close to the cliff-like sides and had them hugging the steep slopes as they walked.

'This is the harracks' porch,' she said. 'Our knowledge stretches no further, but we know this is the beginning of their domain. We must take great care.'

From then on, they grew to dread every stone-fall and constantly craned their necks up, fearfully expecting hidden foes to reveal themselves in ambush. Rounding a bend in the valley, they saw that the valley did not stretch on unimpeded for ever, as it had at first seemed, but was filled with a great narrow ridge, tall and sharp as a ship's prow. Shard-like, and obsidian-dark, it virtually cut the great rounded trough into two smaller valleys. Two branches of the Paraphir opened out, rushing either side of the ridge.

A bitingly cold wind rushed down from the mountains to greet them, and they felt the temperature plummet. With the wind came fresh clouds and new rain, icy cold this time. Their discomfiture soon turned to concern as the rain started to harden into snow.

They trudged onwards, sometimes leaning acutely to keep making progress against the wind. The vicious precipitation stung their faces and any other patch of flesh left exposed. None of their voices had been raised above murmurs for days now, but Curillian had to shout into Sin-Serin's ear just to be heard.

'Which side of this ridge ought we to go?' The wood-elf seemed unsure. She, too, shouted to make her response audible.

'I do not know – it is likely that any path up this valley will take us to the stone city.'

The king made his decision for her.

'We go left.'

Roujeark grew more and more miserable – the snow showed little sign of letting up, and if anything the air seemed to grow colder, making his throat and nostrils smart. His feet were well-shod, but even so he began to feel them grow damp. Curillian led them now, since Sin-Serin had come to the limit of her knowledge. Desperate to gain some shelter from the terrible wind, the king led them to the western side of the left-hand valley. There they were sheltered from the worst onslaught, and found a narrow path cutting up the rock-face. Barely broad enough to walk on, it seemed to have been purposefully created, but so many rocks, fallen from the heights above, littered the way that it was hard to be sure.

They forged up for as long as their strength held out, and then they were forced to stop. They made the most of a little overhang to shelter from the snow and minimise the risk of being struck by falling stones. They swept out the worst of the encroaching snow and laid out blankets. Their wet cloaks they took off and fastened to the overhang as crude windbreaks, replacing them with spare dry cloaks. Roujeark huddled down, shivering, and found himself between two different conversations. To his left, the king and the elf debated in low tones.

'This is a fierce storm for early *Pleuviel*, anyone would think we had set off in winter. The snow is already shin-deep on the track ahead, it must have been snowing here for some time,' the king surmised.

'Snowstorms can strike at any time in the mountains. It may shelter us from the harracks,' Sin-Serin replied. 'But it will be perilous as we climb higher. You may find that the weather is a worse enemy to you and your comrades than any stone-foot.'

On his right, several of the guards were grumbling, teeth chattering, as they huddled together and tried to keep warm.

'Coming up here was a fine idea, wasn't it? Hope our bloomin' guide knows where she's taking us.'

'Look at her there in her tunic and thin cloak, hardly affected by the cold. Maybe she doesn't feel it?'

'Or maybe she's too proud to show weakness in front of us…'

'She's magic, just like that elf-lady back in the forest. It'll be her magic keepin' her warm.'

'Well why doesn't she bloody well share the goods?'

As if to take herself away from their envious looks, Sin-Serin disappeared off into the snow, and Curillian ducked under the overhang to join them.

'Whatever magic she has, she isn't using it right now.' Apparently he had overheard, or guessed, their conversation. 'Elven powers are less potent up here in the mountains, just as the harracks are weaker when out of their element; any attempt to use unnatural abilities here would send an unmistakeable signal to watchers.'

Roujeark looked up at those words, but the idea vanished just as soon as it had appeared – he was too cold to think about any magic.

'Right now,' the king went on, 'she is simply scouting ahead. If she appears to be less susceptible to the cold than us, it is simply because of the natural grace bestowed on elven constitutions. It was the same with men once, long ago, before they turned away from Prélan and forfeited many of His blessings. Now, though, try to get some sleep, we'll move off before dawn.'

True to the king's word, Lancoir roused them all while it was still dark. The barest glimpse around their improvised curtains told them it was still snowing, and that it had accumulated deeply on the narrow path outside. They awoke deeply stiff and unspeakably cold. It took a lot of stamping and flexing before Roujeark could even feel his fingers and toes. They moved off carefully, practically wading through the snow, knowing that even a slight miscalculation could send them sliding down the sheer slope to their right. Sin-Serin was back with them, but if she had gleaned any particular insights on her reconnaissance, she did not share it with them.

Roujeark was no longer merely miserable, just deeply worried. A child of the mountains, he had never known exposure like this. His experiences of snow had been limited to brief forays, and during the heavy stuff he and his father had kept snug inside next to the fire. He was not sure how much longer he could last in conditions like these. Full springtime might be burgeoning down on the plains below, but up here in the mountains winter could re-exert itself whenever its capricious mood took it. Up ahead, he heard one of the guards complaining to Lancoir.

'Why don't we go back? We'll die in this snow without shelter or fire…' Lancoir, though, was unmoved.

'We will not go back. We will make use of this snow for as long as we can. Endure it or be left behind.' Whatever discomfort he himself was feeling, Lancoir, tougher than all of them, was ruthless in dragging the others along with him.

And so they plunged on, braving the snow as best they could. Several times they heard ominous rumblings above them and were soon after showered with snow falling down from the cliff. On one such occasion, Aleinus, the first volunteer, was nearly knocked off the path and into thin air, prevented only by the steady hand of Lancoir, who reached out and caught him.

After an interminable stretch of time, their path seemed to bring them above the level of the trough-valley's rim, for the ice-sheened rock wall on their left gave out. Shaking with cold, Roujeark was dimly aware of gentler slopes stretching away into a blurry distance. All was white here, covered in snow deeper than any they had yet come across. An ill-judged step brought the snow up to his waist, and he had to be tugged out by two of the guards. He could no longer feel the deadly burn in his limbs, and an eerie numbness started to settle over his body like a suffocating blanket. He lost all awareness of where the others were in relation to himself. He barely heard the latest rumble, although it was louder than the ones before. A deep thrumming built up in his ears, soon accompanied by waves of crunching, coming rapidly nearer. Too late he looked left and his vision was filled with a powdery juggernaut. His feet were swept out from under him, his mouth and nose filled with snow and he instantly lost sight of his companions. Terrified and panicking, he was carried along, now submerged in the snow, now just gasping clear. He was turned over and over and around until finally he came to a halt, thoroughly disorientated. By great luck, in his final position he was only covered by a thin film of snow. Scrabbling frantically at it he broke through and glimpsed the muffled grey of the world above. Fleeting relief was soon swamped by a lethargic blackness which stole over him. In the last few seconds before losing consciousness, he heard soft feet crunching near him, and then, as his eyelids slammed shut, a pale shadow reaching down to him.

Character List

Characters listed in alphabetical order, with a syllabic guide to pronounciation and short description for each entry.

ALEINUS (Ah-lee-nus) – Armist, member of Curillian's Royal Guards

ANDIL (An-dil) – Armist, Royal Guardsman; native to the Phirmar

ANTAYA (An-tie-ah) – Armist, member of Curillian's Royal Guards

ANTRUPHAN (An-truh-fan) – Armist, architect to King Curillian

ARAMIST (Ara-mist) – Armist, younger brother of Curillian who died young

ARDIR (Ar-deer) – Angelic messenger of Prélan, usually taking elven form

ARIMAYA (Ar-im-aya) – Armist, late king of Maristonia; grandfather of Curillian

ARTON/CARDANOR (Car-da-nor) – Armist, duke of Arton who acted as regent in Curillian's absence

ATELLIA (A-tell-ee-ah) – Armist, servant-girl working as a masseuse in the duke of Welton's palace; a favourite of Lancoir's

CAREA (Sah-ree-ah) – Elf, princess of the wood-elves

CARÉYSIN (Car-ay-sin) – Armist, army tracker and expert archer

CARION (Cah-ree-on) – Elf, noble wood-elf, father of Dácariel

CARMEN (Car-men) – Armist, queen of Maristonia and wife of Curillian

COMMANGEN (Coh-man-gen) – Armist, clerk in the Royal Library

CURILLIAN (Su-rill-ee-an) – Armist, king of Maristonia and husband of Carmen

CYRON (Ky-ron) – Armist, member of Curillian's Royal Guards

DÁCARIEL (Dah-sah-ree-ell) – Elf, queen of Tol Ankil, niece of Carea and mother of the triplets Sin-Solar, Sin-Tolor & Sin-Serin

DAULASTIR (Daw-luh-stee-ah) – Armist, Lord High Chancellor under King Mirkan. He murdered his master and usurped the throne of the young Curillian, before later being overthrown by the prince when he returned from exile

DUBARNIK (Do-bar-nick) – Armist, conjuror and father of Roujeark

EDRIST (Ed-rist) – Armist, member of Curillian's Royal Guards

FINDOR (Fin-dor) – Armist, member of Curillian's Royal Guards

FIRWAN (fir-wan) – Armist, former King of Maristonia and ancestor of Curillian

GAEON (Guy-on) – Armist, tutor to Prince Téthan

GANNODIN (Gan-no-din) – Armist, general of the elite 1st Legion, garrisoned in Mariston

GERENDAYN (geh-ren-dane) – Wood-elf, antiquary and gatherer of news

HAROTH (Hah-roth) – Armist, member of Curillian's Royal Guards

HORUISTAN (hor-uh-stan) – Armist, general of the 15th legion

ILLYIR (Ill-year) – Armist, duke of Welton; cousin to Curillian

KULOTHIEL (Koo-low-thee-ell) – Man, Head of the League of Wizardry and Keeper of Oron Amular

KURUNDAR (Kuh-run-dar) – Man, sorcerer from Urunmar, brother to Kulothiel

LANCEARON (Larn-sa-ron) – High-elf, king of Ithrill and former Silver Emperor

LANCOIR (Larn-swa) – Armist, Captain of the Royal Guards

LIONENN (Lee-oh-nen) – Armist, army tracker and expert archer

LITHAN (Lee-than) – Elf, king of Kalimar

MANRION (Man-ree-on) – Armist, member of Curillian's Royal Guards

MELNOVA (Mel-no-va) – Armist, celebrated female poet of Maristonia

MIRKAN (Mur-kan) – Armist, prior king of Maristonia; father and predecessor of Curillian

NADIHOAN (Nad-ee-ho-an) – Alias of Curillian during the exile in his youth

NORSCINDE (Nor-sind) – Armist, member of Curillian's Royal Guards

OPHRYIOR (Off-ree-or) – Armist, Lord High Chancellor of Maristonia; Curillian's chief minister

OTAKEN (O-tah-ken) – Armist, general in the Maristonian army

PIRON (Peer-on) – Armist, junior officer of the third cohort of The Royal Guards; second-in-command to Surumo

PRÉLAN (Pray-larn) – God, deity of the elves and all believing folk. Prélan is one and the same as the Triune God of Christianity. He reveals Himself differently to the inhabitants of Astrom than He has to us on Earth.

ROUJEARK (Roo-jark) – Armist, a gifted young magician; son of Dubarnik. The second syllable, 'jeark' is pronounced similarly to the South African forename 'Jacques', with an accented first vowel; not like the flat-vowelled English 'Jack' or 'Jake'.

RUTHARTH (Roo-tharth) – Correct pronunciation of the elvish form of Roujeark's name

RUTHION (RUE-THEE-ON) – Alias of Curillian during his service to the Silver Empire

SIN-SERIN (Sin-seh-rin) – Elf, princess of Tol Ankil, sister of the brothers Sin-Solar and Sin-Tolor

SIN-SOLAR (Sin-so-lar) – Elf, prince of Tol Ankil

SIN-TOLOR (Sin-toe-lore) – Elf, prince of Tol Ankil and brother of Sin-Solar

SURUMO (Suh-roo-mo) – Armist, commanding officer of the third cohort of The Royal Guards

TEKKA (Tech-ah) – Pony, erstwhile mount and companion of Roujeark in his youth

TÉTHAN (Tay-than) – Armist, prince of Maristonia; son and heir of Curillian

THEAMACE (Theam-ace) – Horse, favourite mount of Curillian

THERENDIR (Theh-ren-deer) – Elf, king of the wood-elves, father of Carea

TORLAS (Tor-las) – Elf, prince and swordsmith who forged the Sword of Maristonia for King Armista

UTARION (You-tah-ree-on) – Armist, member of Curillian's Royal Guards

Follow Michael J Harvey on social media:

Facebook.com/worldofastrom

Twitter: @worldofastrom

Instagram: @worldofastrom

Website: worldofastrom.com

Find out more on goodreads.com by scanning the QR code below with your smartphone:

Printed in Great Britain
by Amazon

76182392R00119